"What's the matter, Justin?"

Mary looked directly into his eyes. "You appear to be annoyed," she continued. "Don't you want me to do Mr. Todd's typing?"

Justin's expression was cold. "At last you've actually caught up on that point."

Mary felt nonplussed. "Please tell me why."

"Because I feel sure that there's more to you than meets the eye. I now believe you came here with a purpose. To be blunt, I don't trust you."

Miriam MacGregor began writing under the tutelage of a renowned military historian, and produced articles and books—fiction and nonfiction—concerning New Zealand's pioneer days, as well as plays for a local drama club. In 1984 she received an award for her contribution to New Zealand's literary field. She now writes romance novels exclusively and derives great pleasure from offering readers escape from everyday life. She and her husband live on a sheep-and-cattle station near the small town of Waipawa.

Books by Miriam MacGregor

HARLEQUIN ROMANCE

2931—RIDER OF THE HILLS
2996—LORD OF THE LODGE
3022—RIDDELL OF RIVERMOON
3060—MAN OF THE HOUSE
3083—CARVILLE'S CASTLE
3140—MASTER OF MARSHLANDS
3225—THE INTRUDER

THE ORCHARD KING
Miriam MacGregor

Harlequin Books

TORONTO • NEW YORK • LONDON
AMSTERDAM • PARIS • SYDNEY • HAMBURG
STOCKHOLM • ATHENS • TOKYO • MILAN
MADRID • WARSAW • BUDAPEST • AUCKLAND

Original hardcover edition published in 1992
by Mills & Boon Limited

ISBN 0-373-03255-2

Harlequin Romance first edition March 1993

THE ORCHARD KING

CHAPTER ONE

MARY stood in the citrus orchard. She had not meant to wander quite so far among the globe-shaped trees, and as she gazed up at the ripe oranges contrasting vividly against their dark green foliage she recalled her mother's words.

'It's an Eden with oranges instead of apples,' Elizabeth Kendall had said when describing her old home. 'And beyond the oranges are areas of grapefruit, lemons, mandarins and tangelos.'

'Blossom time must be really something,' Mary had murmured.

'It is—especially as the east coast climate of New Zealand's North Island is so suitable for growing citrus fruit.'

And then Elizabeth's next words echoed in her ears. 'Now remember—don't be tempted to go into the place. Just drive past while taking a quick peep at the general layout.'

'I'd love to walk among the trees,' Mary had said, a wistful note creeping into her voice.

'I wouldn't advise it.' Elizabeth's tone had become abrupt. 'You might meet my father. He'll throw you out on your ear just as he threw me out twenty-five years ago.'

'He won't know who I am,' Mary had protested.

'No? I wouldn't be too sure about that.' Elizabeth had paused to eye her daughter critically. 'You're so similar to myself at your age it's positively ridiculous. If I hadn't put on a little weight we'd be exactly the same build. We have the same type of creamy complexion and dark blue eyes. Your hair is as wavy as my own, and is shoulder-length, which is the way I wore mine when I was twenty-two.' She had given a sudden laugh. 'He'll think he's seeing a ghost. He'll go berserk.'

'Perhaps he's mellowed,' Mary had suggested.

Her mother had snorted. '*Him?* Mellowed? That'll be the day! No, my dear. The nature of a man does not change. So be warned. Stay well clear of your grandfather's domain.'

But Mary had not stayed clear. Curiosity had got the better of her when, having driven several miles along back country roads out of Gisborne, she found herself faced by a large sign at the entrance of the property. 'Valencia', it stated in bold letters. She took a deep breath. *Valencia*—she'd heard the name so many times.

And then she was gripped by a sensation of satisfaction. At last she was looking at the place about which she had heard so much—the place she had yearned to see for so long—the place where her mother had spent her childhood and had grown up. But although she could see the trees she was unable to see the house—and this was most disappointing.

She must see the house, Mary had decided. But to do so meant driving the length of the avenue, which was bordered by tall casuarinas, or she-oaks as they were better known. The shelterbelt of trees with their drooping, feathery, bronzy green needles seemed to offer a feeling of home because there were so many of them in Australia—but this was New Zealand, she reminded herself, and the elderly man living at the end of the avenue was unlikely to offer a welcoming hand of friendship, especially if he guessed her identity.

Staring along the length of the avenue, Mary had felt apprehension creeping up on her. Thoughts of her grandfather banished all desire to approach the house, but at least she could take a closer peep at the trees near the entrance, and perhaps even walk among them. The decision made, she nosed the car near the cattle-grid, then walked through a gap at the end of the she-oaks.

And now, having penetrated further than she had intended, a feeling of unreality came over her, causing her to wonder if this could be a dream. At the far end of a row she could see a long-armed orchard appliance which enabled fruit to be gathered from the tree-tops, and she could hear the faint sound of voices coming from people who picked the fruit.

She stood still, listening to their laughter, and then her attention was caught by the sight of so many oranges lying in the long grass. She bent and picked up a large one, and as she did so the surrounding stillness was shattered by a male voice that echoed irritation as it shouted at her.

'Hi, there—what are you doing at this end of the row? Why aren't you with the other pickers?'

Startled, she swung round to find herself confronted by a tall man whose athletic form would have made him the pride of any rugby team. His face was handsome and would be even more so when it lost the scowl that now marred its regular features. Who was he? she wondered, placing his age at about thirty-two. Definitely not her grandfather, who, according to Mother, owned the orchard. Did that bossy tone indicate that he was an overseer and in charge of the pickers?

Forcing a smile, she said politely, 'I'm just looking—thanks.'

'Are you indeed?' His sensuous mouth twisted as his dark grey eyes swept a glance over her blue knife-pleated skirt and matching jersey with its high collar. 'You're not one of the pickers, as I at first thought. They're all wearing jeans. So who are you and what are you doing here?' The dark grey eyes narrowed thoughtfully as they stared at the orange in her hand.

She dropped the fruit with a guilty air then glared at him in defiance. 'I'm not a thief—if that's what you're thinking,' she snapped, her chin tilting upward as a flush crept into her cheeks.

His jaw tightened. 'No? You wouldn't be the first to sneak in through that gap in the she-oaks,' he rasped.

'You'd deny a person a few of these dozens lying on the ground?' she demanded scathingly.

'Not at all. But do they take them from the ground? Oh, no—they strip the trees instead. The fruit on the ground could be bruised—as you probably know.'

She spoke icily. 'If I'd come to steal your precious oranges I'd have brought a bag, but as you can see—I haven't. I haven't even a pocket.'

'And you haven't any up your jumper?' he queried lazily, his eyes resting upon the small mounds of breasts beneath the blue jersey.

'Of course not,' she gasped, her flush deepening as his gaze remained fixed, until it lifted again to her face, and he then continued to regard her in silence.

Unaware of the attractive picture she made, she returned his gaze unflinchingly. The warmth of the October sun had given a shining lustre to the dark tendrils surrounding her face, and the deep blue of her eyes had taken on a startling depth as, shadowed by black lashes, they reflected the ultramarine of her jersey.

'Who are you?' he demanded again.

'My name is Mary.'

'Of "Mary, Mary, quite contrary" fame?'

A dimple flashed in her cheek. 'You're echoing my mother,' she said demurely while becoming conscious of muscles rippling beneath his open-neck shirt where the V revealed a triangle of short dark hairs.

His next words still held disbelief. 'So Mary is—just looking. Is she unaware that she's trespassing?'

'I'm afraid I didn't think about it. I—I just needed to see the trees,' she admitted lamely.

He frowned as a gleam of suspicion crept into his eyes. 'Are you saying you needed to learn the layout of the orchard? Does this mean you were actually—casing the joint, as they say?'

'Don't be stupid,' she snapped, bristling with anger.

'I'm not being stupid,' he retorted sharply. 'It's been done before. A person of innocent appearance comes during daylight hours to decide upon the best entrance to be made at night. By morning a truckload of fruit has vanished.'

Her eyes widened as she glared at him. 'Please understand that your oranges are quite safe from me.'

'I'm glad of that. I wouldn't like to discover you to be a thief.'

Frustrated, she raised her voice. 'Stop using that word in connection with me. Can't you understand I merely wanted to look at the trees?'

'Have you never seen a citrus orchard before today?'

'No.' Her eyes were drawn to his lustrous black hair.

'In that case you must be a stranger to Gisborne, where there are so many—yet somehow I feel I've seen you before.'

She shook her head. 'I think that's impossible because I've just come over from Australia,' she explained, without knowing why she was admitting to this fact. Then she went on, 'I live in a Sydney suburb where there are only streets and houses, and all this is so different. I was passing and saw the notice at the gate. It made me stop to have a look. It's all so beautiful,' she finished with a sigh.

Her last words appeared to please him, causing a grin to soften the hard lines about his mouth, but rather than admit it he said in a dry tone, 'The trees will be delighted to hear you say so. They adore being admired.'

She fell in with his mood. 'You talk to the trees?'

'Of course.' He moved to lay a hand on a branch. 'Hi, you—do you hear what the lady says? Give her an orange.' Then, plucking two large ones, he handed them to her.

She flushed with pleasure. 'Oh—thank you——'

'Now, if you'll be good enough to move your car you'll stop blocking my exit.'

She was contrite. 'I'm sorry—I meant to stop for only a few seconds to take a quick peep, but the trees acted like magnets that drew me further in.'

He made no reply as they walked towards the gap in the she-oaks, and as they passed through it she saw that his utility truck was parked at the end of the drive, unable to leave it because of her own car. The tray of the small truck was laden with plastic bags, each one bulging with oranges.

The sight of so many oranges drew an exclamation from Mary. 'They are going to market?' she queried.

'Not this lot. They're going to a depot to be sold on behalf of the Boy Scouts. Fund-raising, you understand.'

'You mean—you're giving them away?'

He shrugged. 'I like to do my bit. I was once a Boy Scout. However, I dare say they can spare you a couple of bags.'

She looked at him doubtfully. Were they his to hand to a stranger in this nonchalant manner—or did they belong to her grandfather? But apparently the question had not occurred to him because he lifted two bags from the pile, carried them across the iron-barred cattle-grid and placed them in the grey Honda she'd left nosed into the entrance.

Gratefully, she said, 'Thank you, Mr—er—I'm afraid I don't know your name.'

'King,' he supplied. 'Justin King.' He opened the car door for her then asked abruptly, 'Are you genuinely interested in seeing a citrus orchard?'

'Yes.' Especially this one, she added to herself.

He looked at her thoughtfully then said, 'The pickers are almost ready to finish for the day. They've been at work on the oranges, but if you come at an earlier hour tomorrow you can see them harvesting the grapefruit.'

Mary's surge of excitement was rapidly controlled as she spoke in a calm voice. 'You're sure your—er—employer won't object if you show me round the place?'

He chuckled. 'Actually—I just do as I please.'

'How nice for you.' Again she looked at him doubtfully. According to Mother, people associated with Grandfather did not do as they pleased. They toed the line—otherwise they went down the road. Then she went on, 'Well—thank you. I'd be most interested to see that thing at the end of the row in action.'

'You mean the lifter that enables us to grab the top fruit? Without it we'd lose a lot when they fall and become bruised. Come about mid-afternoon.'

'Only if my parents aren't using the car,' she said as this possibility struck her, then she added quickly, 'And only on condition that you're no longer mad because you found me trespassing in the orchard.'

'Who says I'm mad with you?' His tone had become bored.

'You made it more than clear,' she said, backing the grey Honda towards the roadway, then she smiled to soften the words. After all, he'd given her oranges—and Mother would be more than delighted. Despite her antagonism they might even stir nostalgia and soften her attitude, Mary thought hopefully, visualising herself placing a bag in her mother's arms with the words, 'Here you are—oranges from the Valencia.'

Events had a strange way of coming to pass, she thought as she drove towards the house at Gisborne's Wainui Beach. Earlier in the afternoon she had spoken to her mother with quiet determination when she had said, 'I'm taking a drive to see if I can find the Valencia. Care to come with me?'

'Certainly not.' Elizabeth Kendall's mouth had tightened as her reply had been snapped abruptly. At forty-nine she still retained a youthful appearance which enabled her to look more like Mary's older sister than her mother.

Mary had looked at her thoughtfully before saying, 'Don't you think it's time to let bygones be bygones? After all, he is your father.'

'That's right—my very dear father who threw me out because I married the man I loved——'

'The man who was found to be sadly lacking in every respect,' Mary had cut in to point out gently, the statement being a reminder that the marriage had been a disaster.

'That doesn't alter the situation,' Elizabeth had returned acidly. 'At the time I was deeply in love with Alan Healey. I didn't know he was a womaniser and that he had bouts of heavy drinking. But Father had his suspicions about these facts. He despised Alan.'

'Didn't you tell me he had somebody else in view for you?' Mary had queried, going over previous conversations with her mother.

Elizabeth had sighed. 'Yes, he was keen for me to marry the son of another Gisborne orchardist—a neighbour, actually—his idea being to leave the Valencia in capable hands when he was no longer hale and hearty.'

'I can see what he had in mind,' Mary had admitted.

'Can you indeed?' Elizabeth had snapped wrathfully. 'Can you also see that he was more concerned for the future of his precious orchard than for the happiness of his only daughter?'

'Mother, I'm sure he must've been concerned——'

'Rubbish! The orchard came first.'

Mary avoided further argument on this point by saying, 'So, instead of a wedding reception among trees laden with orange blossom, you eloped with Alan Healey.'

'And was told never to show my face again,' Elizabeth retorted bitterly. 'So *please*—during our stay in Gisborne don't you *dare* ask me to go near the Valencia. My father rejected me, and I intend to remain rejected—unless he comes to me first.'

Mary's voice had taken on a tone of pathos. 'Mother, it's *years* ago. He's an old man. He might *need* you.'

Elizabeth had snorted. '*Him*? Need *me*? That's most unlikely. He'll never need anyone apart from his own stubborn self.'

Mary had taken a deep breath. 'And that makes two of you, Mother. I think you're both as bad as each other,' she accused.

As she drove through Gisborne city and headed towards Wainui Beach her thoughts switched to the man in the orchard. 'Are you married, Justin King?' she asked aloud, safe in the knowledge that no one could hear the words. 'Have you an orange belle hanging on every utterance you make? Masculinity such as your own should bring the girls running from all directions.'

She thought of the utility truck laden with oranges to be sold in aid of the Scouting Movement, then glanced at the colourful bags of fruit lying beside her on the passenger seat. 'You're a generous man, Justin King,' she continued to nobody in particular. 'So long as the fruit is yours to give away. Or does it really belong to my grandfather? I can't say he sounds like one who *gives*.'

When she reached home Mary did not place the bags in her mother's arms as she had planned; instead she laid them on the kitchen table without comment.

But Elizabeth was unable to remain silent. Staring at the oranges, she said, 'You met your grandfather? He gave these to you?'

'No. They were given to me by a man named Justin King who appeared to be working in the orchard. Have you ever heard of him, Mother?' The question came casually.

Elizabeth shook her head. 'No—but you must remember there's been no communication between Father and myself since he cut me out of his life.'

Mary sighed. 'He doesn't even know of my existence. I'm his only grandchild and—and it makes me feel sad.'

Elizabeth spoke briskly. 'You can stop fretting about it because I doubt that he could care less. As far as he's concerned I'm still Mrs Alan Healey, therefore I no longer exist. Personally, I consider you'd be wise to forget about the Valencia—just as I've had to forget about the place.'

'I'm going there again tomorrow,' Mary admitted quietly. 'Justin King has invited me to see the pickers at work.'

Elizabeth's brows rose. 'You talked enough for him to do that? Did you tell him who you are?'

'Certainly not. Nor do I intend to admit I'm the daughter of the daughter.'

'I doubt that he's ever heard of the daughter,' Elizabeth sighed. 'Mine will be the name that's never mentioned for fear of being struck dead.'

Mary hesitated while looking at her mother reflectively, then she asked, 'Have you ever felt you should've swallowed your pride and returned to New Zealand after Alan's death?'

'Definitely not.' Elizabeth's tone was emphatic. 'If I had done so I wouldn't have met your father—and you wouldn't be as you are. Now, then—this evening we'll have chopped orange for dessert, and tomorrow I'll bake an orange cake. Did I ever tell you that Gisborne is famous for its sweet oranges?'

'*Ad nauseam*,' Mary murmured. Was it also famous for handsome individuals like Justin King? she wondered, recalling how the sun had glinted on hair as dark as her own. The sun had also caused those tiny white lines at the corners of his dark grey eyes, she supposed, and had tanned his complexion sufficiently to give him the appearance of an outdoor man. A girl met few such men when living near the heart of Sydney, she realised with a wistful sigh.

The next afternoon found Gisborne living up to its reputation for being a place of warm sunshine. Warm enough, Mary decided, to discard yesterday's jersey and skirt for a dress of lighter weight. The fact that it was also blue

did not concern her because she wore so much of it.
Blue was her colour, and she was well aware that it made
her eyes look like sapphires. She also took extra care
with her make-up, and as she reached for the car keys
lying in a dish on the dresser she knew her mother was
sending anxious glances towards her.

'Is something the matter, Mother?' she felt compelled
to ask.

'Not at all, dear—except that I can't help wondering
why this Mr King is breaking into his work to show you
over the orchard. From what you've told me the brevity
of your meeting doesn't seem to warrant a guided tour.'

'He's probably just being kind,' Mary said, recalling
Justin's generosity to the Boy Scout Association.
'Strangely, he seemed to think he's seen me before, but
of course that's impossible.'

Elizabeth chuckled. 'It's your grandfather who'll think
he's seen you before. He'll probably fall down in a fit.'

'From all you've told me I'd say he's too tough to do
anything so silly.' Then, changing the subject, she asked,
'Where's Daddy?'

'In the dining-room making a list of everything in this
house. It's quite a task.'

Mary found him sitting before sheets of paper spread
over the table. She kissed the grey hair at his temple,
then nodded dutifully when told to drive carefully. A
short time later she was heading towards Gisborne, then
left the city behind her as she sped along country roads
towards the Valencia. A slight skid in loose metal forced
her to reduce speed to a more sedate pace, and she then
began to chide herself. 'What's your hurry? It's possible
he's forgotten you're coming.'

The thought continued to nag at her as she drove over
the cattle-grid and made her way along the avenue of
sheltering she-oaks. At its end she found an extensive
gravel yard spread before a large packing shed which
stood a short distance from a wide-fronted single-
storeyed house.

Justin emerged from the shed as she switched off the motor. He glanced at his watch then raised dark brows. 'Three o'clock exactly. Are you always so punctual—or were you especially anxious to look at this place?'

She looked at him doubtfully, noticing that his eyes held an unfathomable expression while his tone betrayed a hint of irony. Then, ignoring the latter part of his question, she said, 'One learns to be punctual when one has a bus to catch each morning.'

She then waited for him to pursue the subject of her work, but he showed no interest, therefore she said hesitantly, 'If it's inconvenient I can go home.'

'No. It's just that I can't help wondering why a city girl is so madly interested in a back country citrus orchard.'

She forced a smile that revealed white even teeth. 'Contrast of lifestyle,' she said, snatching at the first thought to come into her head, then felt relief when he changed the subject.

'The pickers are having their afternoon tea break, but we'll have ours at the house.'

The house—she was about to see inside her mother's old home? This was more than Mary had hoped for, but the flutter of excitement subsided rapidly when he led her round the corner of the house and she saw that tea would be served on a veranda table.

An elderly man sat at the table, a portable typewriter before him. His iron-grey hair was matched by bushy eyebrows, while a grey moustache sat beneath an aquiline nose, the latter feature giving his face an undeniable arrogance. Even from a distance his chin seemed to jut with determination as he poked at the typewriter, and this, Mary realised, was her first view of her grandfather.

As they went up the veranda steps he glanced up, then appeared to freeze as though gripped by a sudden state of shock. His blue eyes widened, his jaw sagged, and he rose unsteadily to his feet while continuing to gape at Mary in a bewildered manner. And as his hands gripped the edge of the table he leaned forward for a closer view, then he sank back into his chair.

Justin sensed that something was wrong. He hastened to the older man's side and laid a hand on his shoulder. 'What's the matter, Rex? You look as if you've just seen a ghost.' Then, turning to Mary, he made the introduction. 'This is Rex Todd—but I'm afraid I've no idea of your name.'

'Kendall,' she supplied, feeling secretly amused. 'Spinster.'

'Ah.' His tone held satisfaction. 'Rex, this is Miss Mary Kendall—the young lady I found in the orchard.'

Rex Todd continued to gape at Mary in silence.

Justin looked at him anxiously. 'What's the matter, Rex? Haven't you seen a pretty girl before? You look as if you've just become president of the Gawping Society.'

Rex appeared to pull himself together. 'Mary, you say?'

'Plain as any name can be,' she replied lightly, quoting from an old song.

'It's a grand old name,' Rex said with decision. 'My late wife was Mary. Actually—you remind me of her.'

The words surprised Mary. She had expected him to have been reminded of his daughter—but apparently he'd brainwashed himself into erasing all memory of her mother. However, further discussion was curtailed when a comfortably built woman with a pleasant face came out on to the veranda. She carried a teapot, which she added to the cups and saucers on a tray already resting on the table.

Justin introduced Mary to her. 'Laura—this is Mary Kendall.' Then, turning to Mary, he added, 'Laura is Mrs Todd—Rex's wife.'

The last words came as a shock to Mary. *Grandfather had married again*? Of course he had needed someone to take care of him over the last twenty-five years—but Mother would be most interested to learn that she had a stepmother. She smiled inwardly at the thought of delivering the news.

She then watched with interest as the older woman poured the tea. Laura Todd was a kindly person, she decided, judging her to be about sixty despite the lack of lines on her face. She liked the way her grey hair set in neat waves, and she noticed that her grey eyes were similar in colour to Justin's.

And then Justin delivered another surprise. 'Laura is my aunt,' he informed Mary. 'She is my mother's sister.'

Mary made a polite sound, but she was more interested in her grandfather, who, she realised, was having difficulty in keeping his eyes away from her face. To divert his attention she indicated the portable typewriter and the papers beside it. 'You're writing letters?' she asked with a show of polite interest.

'No. I've been talked into writing my memoirs,' he admitted gruffly. 'They're combined with a history of citrus-fruit-growing in the Gisborne district. Getting it typed is my main problem because I can only jab at this infernal machine with one finger.'

'You're doing very well, dear,' Laura assured him kindly.

'I'm not,' he growled. 'I'm making a damned mess of it. I'd like to see a nice professional job, and I suspect there are quite a few spelling errors as well.'

'What's wrong with using a dictionary?' Justin queried.

'The blasted print's too small in the dratted thing,' Rex complained.

'Could I suggest a public typist?' Mary said.

The old man gave a snort of derision. 'Those stupid women can't read my writing,' he grumbled. 'It needs somebody to do the job here——'

'So that he can be on hand to decipher the scrambled hieroglyphs,' Justin put in.

'My writing is not all that bad,' Rex snarled.

An idea had sprung into Mary's head, but she hesitated to voice it too soon. Then, fearing the opportunity would pass, she took courage and said, 'Perhaps I could help you. I can type. I spend my time typing—at least I did before the office closed when my employer went to England.'

'Does this mean you're out of a job?' Justin said.

Mary shrugged. 'Yes—at the moment. But it doesn't matter because it enabled me to come to New Zealand with my parents.' She turned to the older couple with further explanation. 'We live in Sydney, but my father's mother lived in Gisborne at Wainui Beach. She died recently, so my parents have had to cross the Tasman to deal with her house and belongings. Father was her only child.'

Rex's eyes had narrowed. 'So you're an Australian. What sort of work does your father do?'

'He's a dentist,' Mary informed him. 'He's employed a locum while taking time off to attend to Gran's affairs.'

'Aren't you being rather inquisitive, dear?' Laura chided her husband.

'Mary will forgive an old man's curiosity,' he returned calmly. 'Now about this typing——'

Interruption came from Justin, who threw cold water on the idea. 'I don't consider that Mary's time in this country should be monopolised by another typewriter,' he declared abruptly.

She sent him a glance of surprise. 'Really, I wouldn't mind. I—I'd like to help.'

'Why?' The question was shot at her while a mocking glint crept into his eyes. 'You must have a reason for—wanting to help.'

She looked at him blankly. Oh, yes—she had a reason, but not one to be voiced aloud. Here was the golden opportunity to learn to know her grandfather, and to question him about things Mother didn't seem to know. But even as she sought for an answer to Justin's question Laura betrayed amazement.

'Really, Justin—one would imagine you were against Mary giving Rex this assistance.'

'To be honest I'm not keen,' he admitted frankly. 'Mary doesn't know what she'd be letting herself in for,' he added, grinning to soften the words.

'You'll make her think I'm a tyrant,' the old man complained.

'Your reputation is no secret,' Justin reminded him. 'However, we won't go into that. What I'm trying to point out is that there are numerous typists in the district.' He paused, frowning, then said bluntly, 'Rochelle would be willing to make another attempt.'

'Would she, indeed?' Rex's mouth clamped shut in a tight line.

The exchange between the two men had amazed Mary. She had never met an employee who was quite as autocratic and as free of speech towards the boss as Justin was proving to be. Or did the fact that he was Laura's nephew make a difference? And who was Rochelle? she wondered. Obviously someone whose efforts had failed to please, but who was willing to try again—perhaps to impress the handsome Justin King.

The best of luck to you, Rochelle—whoever you are, she offered silently. It's obvious he wants to see you at the typewriter rather than myself, although what he has against me I've yet to fathom. And I do know there's something bugging him about me—not that I care two hoots about it, of course.

In an effort to shrug off the conviction that it really did irritate her she changed the subject by turning to Rex with a question. 'Have you ever tasted those large sweet Queensland mandarins, Mr Todd? Is it possible to grow them here?'

'I'm afraid not,' he admitted regretfully. 'But some of our tangelos are every bit as good. They're sweet and peel like the best mandarins.'

The topic caused Justin to remind Mary that she had come to see the pickers at work. She stood up, but as she was about to leave the veranda Rex spoke to her in a tone that held determination.

His eyes glinting beneath his shaggy brows, he said, 'About this typing—would you be willing to do it for me? You'd be paid.'

She found difficulty in controlling her inner jubilation, and only with an effort was a smile kept from her face as she spoke seriously. 'Actually, I'd love to do it because it would help fill in my time—but payments wouldn't be necessary. A few oranges would be sufficient.'

'Nonsense,' Rex snorted. 'Nobody works for me without payment.'

Glancing at Justin, Mary was in time to see a momentary frown crease his brow, then vanish. So she was right. He did not wish her to do the job. And then another thought struck her, forcing her to say with reluctance, 'Unfortunately there's a snag. It's a matter of transport. The grey Honda I'm driving is not completely at my disposal. It was Gran's car, and my parents need the use of it while attending to her estate. So you see——'

Her words died away as she turned to Justin. Was it her imagination, or did he seem visibly relieved? If so it was short-lived because when Laura spoke her words brought a return of the tension Mary had previously sensed.

'Transport shouldn't be allowed to stand in the way,' the older woman said. 'Surely the solution is obvious. Why not stay with us for a couple of weeks?' she invited warmly. 'You could get the job done without the hassle of driving to and from Wainui, which, after all, is quite a distance.'

'Mary's parents are sure to need her assistance,' Justin pointed out in a tone that was meant to settle matters.

She smiled, shaking her head while hoping the surge of eagerness she felt did not show on her face. 'There's little I can do to help my parents make decisions about everything my grandmother had in her house. Daddy says she was a dreadful hoarder, but Mother says she was a sentimental saver who couldn't bear to part with anything that had been given to her, or that applied to the past.'

Laura nodded. 'We become like that as we grow older,' she said with understanding. 'We cling to the past. So—will you agree to stay with us?'

Mary took a deep breath as she made the decision. 'Yes—I'd like to do that. Would Justin mind fetching me, say, tomorrow?'

She turned to him, hoping to discover a more amiable expression on his face, but he appeared to have lost all interest in the discussion while staring moodily towards the citrus trees.

He doesn't want me to be here, she thought sadly.

And this appeared to be a fact because instead of assuring her that he'd be pleased to fetch her he left the veranda and set off across the lawn towards the orchard.

His action filled Mary with a sudden misgiving, but she sent a brief smile towards the older couple and said, 'I'll see you both tomorrow.' Then she followed Justin, running to catch up with the long strides that carried him towards the trees. As she reached his side she panted, 'What's the matter, Justin? You appear to be annoyed. Don't you want me to do Mr Todd's typing?'

He stopped abruptly, swinging round to face her, his expression cold. 'At last you've actually caught up on that point.'

She was shocked by his words. 'You mean you really don't want me to come here and do that job?'

'That's right.' His voice was like granite. 'When I offered to show you the orchard it did not include a period of living in the house, which I now consider to be most unwise.'

She felt nonplussed. 'Please tell me why,' she quavered.

'Because I feel sure there's more to you than meets the eye. Rex's reaction to the sight of you woke me up to that fact, and I now believe you came here with a purpose. To be blunt, *I don't trust you.*'

'Thank you very much.' His words had been like a slap in the face but she remained calm as she said, 'I'll call it off. I'll tell Mr Todd——' Then she turned to leave him.

His hand on her arm restrained her. 'Don't do that— he'd be most disappointed. I'd prefer you to do the typing as arranged, but at least you know where you stand as far as I'm concerned.'

'I certainly do,' she gritted at him. 'My motive for being here is highly suspect, therefore you have no confidence in me. Right?'

'Right. In the meantime I intend to act as though these facts haven't been laid bare. Now then—shall we look at the pickers?'

CHAPTER TWO

JUSTIN led Mary towards the area where the pickers were busy, and as they walked between the rows of trees he queried in a slightly cool tone, 'Are you always so suddenly generous to a stranger, Mary?'

She sent him a startled glance. 'Generous? I'm afraid I don't know what you mean.'

'This readiness to sacrifice your holiday to type the memoirs of a person you've only just met. I find it somewhat unusual—or is there a motive behind the gesture?'

The latter question, which came casually, was enough to put her on her guard. She must think of a reason for making the offer, she realised, and fortunately she was able to come up with one that was quite genuine. 'I'm becoming rather bored at Wainui,' she admitted. 'There's nothing I can do to assist my parents in making decisions about what to do with Gran's furniture and her cupboards full of linen and china. I need to do something more constructive than just looking at the sea or walking along the beach.'

'So you decided to take a look at a citrus orchard—preferably one a few miles out of Gisborne rather than those that are close at hand,' he added with a hint of irony.

His tone caused her to send him a forced smile. 'My goodness, you do flatter yourself if you imagine this to be the only orchard that has caught my interest. I've stopped the car to look at several.' She paused, then added without knowing exactly why, 'The place next door to this property appears to be nicely laid out.'

'You're becoming discerning?' His tone was now sardonic. 'That happens to be Rochelle's home.'

'Really?' She waited to hear more about Rochelle, but he remained silent, plainly hinting he was not to be drawn.

Instead he returned to her former admission. 'So boredom was your only reason for making this offer to type the memoirs?'

'Not exactly. To be honest I thought it would be an interesting project. The memoirs of some elderly people can be quite revealing—I mean quite *fascinating*,' she amended hastily.

'I doubt that you'll get a complete record in this case,' Justin warned. 'Some of Rex's past is sure to be excluded.'

'For what reason?' she asked with an air of innocence while hiding her disappointment.

'Because some of his memories irritate him,' Justin returned. 'There are events in his life he refuses to discuss, so he's unlikely to allow other people to read about them.'

'In that case his memoirs won't be complete,' Mary pointed out.

'That's so. But it's for him to record or omit as he wishes.'

She put out a tentative feeler. 'I suspect he's a tyrant.'

Justin paused beside a tree before he admitted, 'At one time he had the reputation of being a demanding old devil—but I understand he's mellowed with the years. Life with my aunt has made a difference to him. She's a sweet person.'

Mary found herself losing interest in her grandfather as she looked at Justin and voiced a question. 'And his overseer—is he also a demanding devil?'

The sensuous lips twitched. 'You're referring to me?'

'I haven't met anyone else,' she reminded him.

'Well, now that you mention it I have noticed the raucous chatter diminish when I approach the pickers.

And that means more care being taken as the fruit is removed from the branch.' He paused before sending her a searching glance. 'So what about you? Are you also one who demands?'

'I hope not,' she said, then, not wishing to become involved in a discussion which concerned herself, she reverted to the subject of the pickers. 'I don't see any ladders along this row of trees,' she said, staring along its length.

He followed her gaze. 'Their turn is coming. They're the Wheeny grapefruit which ripen from October to January—the large pale yellow ones that are so full of juice.'

'Then where are the pickers?' she asked, determined to keep the conversation impersonal. 'I can hear them, but I can't see them.'

'They're with the Morrison seedless which ripen from July to October when their skins are golden and their flesh has turned orange.'

They moved towards the sound of voices, which diminished as they drew near, and, noticing the silence that became intense, Mary whispered, 'They know you're coming. Are they afraid of you?'

'I doubt it. Something tells me they're more interested in you,' he returned in a low voice. 'They're not accustomed to the sight of a pretty girl being shown round the orchard.'

She glowed within herself but said, 'Nonsense. They're probably waiting for the overseer to crack his whip.'

'You're saying I look like the proverbial slave-driver?'

'Well—maybe his brother.'

'Thank you for your confidence in my ability to influence and win the friendship of staff.'

She looked at him doubtfully. 'Are you thinking that I've insulted you?'

'Not at all.' The words came crisply, implying that he didn't care what she thought, although his continued frown contradicted his denial.

Mary remained silent, mainly because she didn't know what to say. She regretted her own carelessness and rather tactless words, being well aware that she had no proof of their truth. Nor had she any wish to be on bad terms with her grandfather's overseer, especially if they were to see more of each other in the near future.

Or would she see anything at all of him? she wondered. After all, she would be inside the house while he'd be out in the packing shed or in the orchard. When evening came he'd probably vanish by going home to a wife and child. Then, annoyed to find her thoughts moving in this direction, she shook herself mentally while turning her attention to the activity before her.

The most prominent feature of the scene was a large flat trailer stacked with two layers of grapefruit-filled cases. It was drawn by a tractor, which stood ready to be driven further along the row. Other cases resting on the ground were being filled by the three pickers who stood on ladders while snipping the golden balls hanging among the shining green leaves.

Mary watched as the fruit was carefully snipped from the branches to be placed in a bulging bag that hung from the front of each picker, and while acute concentration appeared to be given to their work she knew that she herself was being observed. It was almost as though it was a rarity for their overseer to conduct a female visitor round the orchard, she thought, then decided that this was probably her imagination.

From the grapefruit they moved to where the trees were laden with lemons, which seemed to decorate the branches like masses of yellow baubles. Then, as they turned into another row, Mary found herself confronted by more oranges than she had ever seen in her life.

The colourful sight caused her to catch her breath, and, standing still to gaze at the sun-ripened fruit, she exclaimed, 'They're so beautiful!'

Justin's smile betrayed satisfaction as he said, 'You should see the rows at blossom time. Each one is a bridal walk while the air is heady with perfume and buzzing with the hum of bees.'

'It must be lovely,' she sighed, recalling her mother's wish for a wedding in the orchard.

'If you're thinking of getting married during blossom time you'd be welcome to hold the affair here,' he invited casually.

She was startled by the suggestion. It was almost as though he had read her thoughts, but of course that was impossible. However, she responded with a smile. 'Thank you—that would be lovely—especially if the rain started falling in torrents. But aren't you forgetting I'm not a native of these parts? My wedding will probably take place in Sydney.'

'Ah—so you are engaged?'

'I didn't say that.'

'But you do have a definite boyfriend?'

'Several of them, all just good friends. I'm not exactly neglected, you understand.' She paused as curiosity caused her to toss the ball into his court. 'Was your own wedding held in the bridal walk, Mr King?' she asked sweetly.

A laugh escaped him. 'My own wedding? No—but it's worth thinking about, if such an event ever occurs—which is most unlikely.'

Mary felt a stir of interest. 'Why is it unlikely, Mr King?'

'Because I prefer to remain free of the female species,' he said, smiling as though to soften any hint of rudeness. Then he added, 'I've had all the experience I need in that direction. As the Scottish people say, women are kittle cattle.'

She turned indignant eyes upon him. 'Kittle cattle? What's that supposed to mean?'

A hard line appeared about his mouth. 'It means they're tricky and require careful handling. Perhaps untrustworthy is a better word. They know all the tricks of the trade.'

Mary was puzzled. 'The trade? What trade, for Pete's sake?'

'The trade of getting everything they want through subtle means of their own. As I said—kittle cattle,' he finished bitterly.

'Poor Mr King—I presume there was someone who let you down and you're judging the rest of the—er—female species by her,' Mary said with perception.

'The episode was enough to teach me a lesson,' he retorted coldly.

'It's a recent occurrence?' she asked quietly.

'No—it's a few years ago before I came into my——' He fell silent for several moments, then finished by saying, 'Before I came to the Valencia.'

'Where you've been wallowing in self-pity ever since.'

He glared at her then snarled, 'I'm not sorry for myself.'

Her eyes were filled with sympathy. 'No? You could've fooled me. It's obvious you're allowing the experience to fester in your throat like a ball of bitterness that should be spat out. Why don't you rid yourself of it?'

'Because I've no wish to do so,' he retorted enigmatically. 'But that's something you wouldn't understand.'

'On the contrary, I understand perfectly,' she said in a voice that was deceptively gentle. 'It keeps you safe. It's your cloak—your protection against all other *kittle cattle*. I can't help wondering what actually happened.'

He shrugged. 'It was a common enough story. We were about to become engaged when she deserted me for a man who had more money than I had at that particular time.'

'It must have been a terrible blow—especially to your pride.'

'At least I managed to live through it, but it won't happen again,' he declared firmly.

'This ghastly trauma happened—how long ago did you say?'

'I didn't say, but it's now ten years ago. And why the devil I'm confiding these details to someone who is virtually a stranger, I'll never know,' he rasped.

'To talk gives relief,' she pointed out.

He went on, 'A short time later my aunt married Rex. I paid them a visit and have been here ever since. Rex and I had something in common because he too had been deserted.'

She frowned, feeling suddenly puzzled. 'Mr Todd—had been deserted?'

'When Laura came to keep house for him he was a widower, but apparently he had a daughter who had left him in the lurch just when he needed care and understanding.'

Mary became very still while making an effort to control her indignation, but at last she was able to ask casually, 'Did you hear what actually happened? Why did she—er—desert him?'

'I'm unaware of the details apart from the fact that she ran away with a fellow who was no good.'

Her brows rose as she sent him a look of wide-eyed enquiry. 'Are you admitting to a male variety of kittle cattle?' The words came innocently.

He ignored her tone as he said, 'According to Rex he was a number-one rat.'

At least she could agree with him on that point, Mary decided, then, wondering if her grandfather's attitude was still as bitter as ever, she asked, 'Where is his daughter now?'

'I've no idea. Her name is never mentioned, and it seems to me that as far as Rex is concerned she's dead.'

Mary controlled the emotions that threatened to make her shake with fury. She took a deep breath as she queried, 'How did he fare without his daughter? I presume that no longer having her at his beck and call must have been most irritating.'

'I understand he had a series of housekeepers, none of them lasting very long until my aunt applied for the position. Since then his old age—plus her companionship—have caused him to mellow. Even his bad temper appears to have disappeared.'

'Perhaps your aunt has made him realise it's the custom for girls to leave their parents when they marry,' Mary suggested drily.

'Does the average girl marry a man for whom her father has no respect—a man her father positively loathes and refuses to have near the place?'

'In that case I doubt that the story of desertion is correct. Are you sure he didn't throw her out for marrying such a man?'

He kicked at a tuft of grass then said with a faintly bored air, 'To be honest I've given it little or no thought. However, if Rex declared his daughter deserted him—I believe him.'

Frustrated, she decided that the topic must be dropped before she began jumping up and down while shouting angry protestations in defence of her mother. How *dared* her grandfather declare he'd been deserted? He was a horrible old man, and now that she had seen the orchard and had met him she felt little desire to have further contact with him.

Justin regarded her with interest. 'You've become quite flushed. Has something upset you?'

Unguardedly she said, 'I'm wondering if I've been too hasty in agreeing to type the memoirs of such a man.'

'It was you who suggested it,' he drawled. 'In fact you appeared to be quite eager to do so. Are you one who goes back on your word?'

'Of course not,' she snapped. 'And don't you dare to drop hints about kittle cattle. I've said I'll do his typing and the job will be done,' she flashed at him.

'Good girl.' His eyes travelled over her face, taking in details of her flawless complexion and the dark, delicately pencilled brows arching above her large blue eyes that were so deep in colour. At last they rested for several long moments upon the curve of her sweetly generous mouth.

His scrutiny made her feel embarrassed, and, searching for words, she said, 'I'm keeping you from your work. He'll have your liver on a dish—and mine too.'

Justin laughed, his mirth transforming his face. 'First he'll have to find a dish large enough for two livers.'

The remark lightened the atmosphere between them. Nevertheless she said seriously, 'I must go home and sort out a few clothes to throw into a case.'

They walked to where her car had been left, and as she took her place behind the wheel she was given a reminder as Justin said, 'See you tomorrow at ten-thirty.'

She gave him the address then added, 'I'll be ready.'

Antagonism against her grandfather vanished as she drove along the avenue of she-oaks. Instead of simmering in her mind it was replaced by the satisfaction of knowing she would see Justin King tomorrow, and as she speeded towards home her mind raked over the dresses hanging in her wardrobe.

And then the problem of what to take was swept aside by the knowledge that her future task must be admitted to her mother. Mother would not be amused, she feared. And she was right.

Elizabeth made no comment when told that her father had remarried, and she listened in silence when Mary told her that Laura was a pleasant person whose influence had caused Grandfather to mellow. 'That I shall believe when—and if ever—I see it,' she said.

'If you'll be reasonable, Mother, it might be sooner than you think,' Mary hinted quietly.

Elizabeth sent her a sharp glance. 'What do you mean? You know perfectly well I've no intention of going near the place—and I trust you're now finished with it.'

'Well—not quite,' Mary admitted. 'I'm going back tomorrow.'

'You can't have the car tomorrow,' Elizabeth informed her in a firm tone. 'Your father and I will be needing it in the morning.'

'That doesn't matter because Justin King, the overseer, will be calling for me. I'll be staying there for a while,' she admitted, dropping the bombshell.

There was a moment's silence while her father lowered his newspaper and her mother's eyes bulged in disbelief. '*Staying* there?' Elizabeth exclaimed reproachfully. 'You actually intend to *stay* at the Valencia? I'd have thought that after the treatment I received it would have been a place to avoid.'

Mary made an effort to ignore her mother's displeasure while going on bravely to explain the typing job. 'Can't you understand——?'

Elizabeth cut in impatiently. 'Oh, yes, I can understand your wish to see the orchard—and even to catch a glimpse of your grandfather. But to *stay* there—and to do his *typing*—well, I can hardly believe it.'

Mary turned appealing eyes towards her father, who had sat in silence during the exchange between herself and her mother. 'What do you think, Daddy? Am I betraying Mother by doing this typing?'

'Certainly not.' Peter Kendall's brown eyes rested upon her with understanding. He was a mild man whose dark hair was well streaked with grey, and although not a garrulous person his brief statements were usually to the point.

'But Mother thinks I'm being disloyal,' Mary persisted sadly.

'That's only a temporary reaction,' he explained. 'When she's given it more thought she'll realise that you are learning about your background and discovering your roots, and that the opportunity to take a good look at them must not be denied. No doubt it'll be the only one you're likely to get, so you'd be wise to make the most of it.'

'Thank you, Daddy. I knew you'd understand,' Mary said gratefully. She felt thankful she'd waited until he was present before revealing her plans. He had a calming influence, whereas her mother had inherited a portion of Grandfather's temper. However, she seldom blew her top in Daddy's presence, Mary reflected while waiting for her father to make further comment on the subject.

He went on, 'This typing will also give you something to do. Your mother knows there's been little to occupy you here, nor have you met anyone with whom to make friends. Maybe you'll meet somebody.'

A vision of Justin King's handsome face rose before her, but she brushed it aside as she said, 'There's more to it than having something to do, Daddy. All my life I've heard about the Valencia, and suddenly I have the opportunity to examine every nook and cranny of the place.'

Peter chuckled. 'Deep in her heart your mother would love to be with you—doing just that. She's probably envious.'

'*I am not*,' Elizabeth exploded vehemently. 'Wild horses wouldn't drag me within a mile of it. And please stop talking as though I'm not here.'

He went on unperturbed. 'And there's something else to remember. Your mother's quarrel with her father is not your quarrel—so just take the old boy as you find him.'

'Well, *really*——' Elizabeth began on an indignant note.

Peter soothed her with an indulgent smile. 'My dear, I can't believe you'd deny Mary this experience. She must learn to decide upon her own course—just as you did when you were her age,' he added slyly.

Elizabeth opened her mouth to protest, then shut it again.

Mary spoke quickly to appease her mother. 'I doubt that it'll be a very long job,' she said, recalling the small pile of papers on the veranda table, then was forced to wonder if there could be more larger piles inside the house.

'You're probably right,' Elizabeth conceded. 'His memoirs will consist of a conglomerate of notes taken from his diaries. He always kept a diary. I wonder how much of the truth was recorded in them?' she added bitterly. 'Perhaps you'll be able to judge for yourself.'

'Perhaps,' Mary agreed. She had not mentioned the word desertion which had cropped up during her conversation with Justin King. In fact, with one exception, she had avoided all mention of his name, fearing that her parents would suspect that he was the real reason for her desire to spend time at the Valencia. Which was ridiculous, of course. It had nothing to do with her grandfather's overseer. It was her grandfather who needed her help.

Elizabeth broke into her thoughts. 'This overseer you mentioned—I must say he's a surprise. My father was always adamant about seeing to details himself. "Don't allow other people to handle your affairs", he used to declare. An overseer of staff was the last thing he would have tolerated. People did as they were told or they were sent down the road.'

Peter sent Mary a glance that held curiosity. 'Am I to understand you intend keeping your mother's identity hidden?'

'That's correct. I'll just be Mary Kendall to him.'

'And of no connection to a young woman who ran away to marry Alan Healey. In that case you'll have to stop referring to him as Grandfather—or you'll let something slip,' Peter warned.

She was startled. 'Yes—you're right. I must be careful. In future I'll refer to him only as Mr Todd.' She took a deep breath, and, unaware of the light in her eyes, she smiled at her parents. 'Now then—I must sort out clothes because tomorrow morning Justin—I mean the *overseer*—will fetch me to do *Mr Todd's* typing.'

As she left the room she noticed her parents send enquiring glances towards each other. However, neither said a word.

Next morning Justin arrived as the living-room clock struck ten-thirty. By that time Peter and Elizabeth had left to attend to estate business in Gisborne, a fact which caused Mary to offer an apology.

'I'm sorry my parents aren't here to meet you, but their first appointment for today was with the solicitor at ten o'clock.' She looked at him thoughtfully, noting the perfect cut of dark green jacket and pale fawn trousers which clung to his narrow hips. Then she asked, 'May I offer you coffee, or must you rush back to the orchard?'

'Coffee would be nice, thank you.' He followed her into the living-room then stood looking at the piles of sheets, towels and pillowcases on the table.

'Mother has been going through Gran's linen,' Mary explained, noticing his interest. 'The house has to be emptied before it can be sold.'

She went through to the kitchen and filled the electric kettle, then became aware that he had followed her. She felt rather than saw his eyes watching every movement she made, and for some unknown reason her hand began to shake as she placed a small jug of creamy milk on the tray, almost causing the liquid to slop over the rim.

Control yourself, dimwit, she chided herself mentally. Remember he's allergic to women. They're untrustworthy, you understand. And then the thought of her own secret gave her a qualm, but she told herself it concerned her grand—*Mr Todd*—rather than his overseer.

Overseer? In some intangible manner the aura of male vitality emanating from this man endowed him with more than overseer status. The ability to see that staff toed the line and that every tree in the orchard produced its full quota of the best quality fruit would surely be his. There was a dominance about him that could not be denied, and Mary felt it seeping through to engulf her, causing her voice to become unsteady.

'We'll have our coffee on the veranda,' she said, annoyed by the tremor in her tone.

'How long have you been in Gisborne?' His deep voice came quietly as he lifted the tray and carried it through the living-room and out to the wicker table and chairs.

'Less than a week,' she admitted. 'When Gran passed away Daddy was fortunate to find a locum at such short notice.'

'And on arrival it took you about five minutes to rush out in search of citrus orchards?' His gaze had become intense, almost as if trying to search out the truth of this question. 'I wonder why you were in such a hurry?' he mused.

She forced a laugh. 'You sound as if you think I had an ulterior motive. The reason is simple. It was a matter of transport. I think I told you we're using Gran's car while we're here, and I knew that if I didn't see a few orchards right smartly I wouldn't be able to see them at all because my parents would need the car.' Did that satisfy him? she wondered. But as his eyes had become hooded she was unable to tell whether or not he believed her.

'You visited her often?' he asked casually.

She saw the trap but was able to say truthfully, 'No. This is my first trip to New Zealand. Gran always crossed the Tasman to us.'

'Why was that?' The question held mild curiosity.

'Because Mother doesn't like——' She stopped abruptly, aware that she had been about to admit that Gisborne held painful memories for her mother. Then, realising that he waited for her to go on, she said, 'Well—actually—Mother doesn't like flying. She declares she sits in terror from when the plane takes off until the moment it touches the tarmac and she can disembark.' At least this was true, she thought, excusing her prevarication.

'She's not the only person who dislikes flying,' he conceded.

'Dear old Gran loved it. We're so glad she made those trips while she was able to do so,' Mary said softly.

His gaze became narrowed as he stared at the distant hilly slopes across the sparkling blue of the bay. 'So— your parents are New Zealanders?'

'Yes.' The response came reluctantly because she had no wish to discuss them with this man.

'Yet you've seen nothing of the country. On the way home I'll take you up Kaiti Hill. It will give you a panoramic view of the city and Young Nick's Head.'

Her eyes widened as she almost quailed visibly. 'Are you saying somebody's head is up there?'

He gave a shout of genuine mirth that cleared his face of any hint of suspicion. 'You'll have to wait until we get there,' he teased. 'We'll consider it to be part of your education.'

Feeling slightly nettled, she said, 'I can't see why you should be interested in my education.'

'Perhaps it's because I'm puzzled about you,' he admitted. 'I'd like to know why you'd take drives along back country roads before viewing nearby places of historic importance. I mean—they're a *must* for every visitor to Gisborne.'

Her shoulders lifted slightly. 'No doubt I'll get round to seeing them sooner or later.'

'Not if you're chained to old Rex's typewriter,' he warned.

His eyes held her own in a hypnotic stare for several long moments, then Mary looked away, fixing her gaze on the tops of tall Norfolk pines and grey-green pohutukawa trees rising above neighbouring houses. There was an astuteness about this man's probing—a perceptive awareness that made her feel uncomfortable. It was almost as though he suspected her of having a special reason for giving a back country drive priority over the viewing of these other sights—as indeed she had.

However, the subject of her priorities was not one she wished to pursue, therefore she stood up hastily and spoke in a slightly reproving tone. 'Shouldn't we be on our way—or would you like more coffee?' she queried as hospitality prevailed.

'Yes, thank you, I'd enjoy another mug of that fine brew,' he drawled lazily.

'You're not concerned about Mr Todd wondering where we are?'

'Not at all—although no doubt he'll be champing at the bit while waiting to see you at work on his memoirs.'

'In that case shouldn't we hurry?' she persisted.

'All in good time,' he said in a leisurely manner, his eyes watching her face.

His scrutiny caused her to snatch the tray and hurry back to the kitchen, where she refilled the two coffee-mugs.

He followed at a slower pace, then startled her by asking, 'Am I right in suspecting you're madly keen to get back to the orchard?'

'No, you're not,' she informed him sharply. 'But there's something about your attitude which suggests you're not keen to take me. Why don't you admit it?'

'I'd be lying if I failed to do so,' he said with what could only be termed brutal frankness.

She stared at him mutely, shaken by his candid reply. 'I believe you've taken a dislike to me,' she said, feeling suddenly perplexed. 'What have I done to have caused it?'

'You've appeared,' he snapped abruptly.

She gaped at him, not quite sure of his meaning. 'I've appeared to what——?'

'I mean you've loomed over the horizon. And now you've arrived.'

'Why should that upset you?' she asked, still quite bewildered.

'I don't know. But it does.' His tone had become terse.

She spoke icily. 'If it weren't for my promise to type the memoirs, I'd tell you to go to hell.'

'But you won't, because you're itching to come to Valencia. On the way we'll leave oranges and lemons at the public hospital.'

'They buy them from you?' she asked, pleased to change the subject from one that revealed his antagonism towards herself.

'Certainly not. It pleases me to make these small donations.'

She stared towards the distant horizon, then found herself unable to resist voicing a question. 'I suppose Mr Todd requests you to take them there?'

He uttered a short laugh. 'Rex? Of course not. I doubt that he's given away much fruit over the years.'

She was shocked by the temerity of his admission. Even if it was in a good cause, it simply wasn't honest to give away fruit that didn't belong to him. A surge of disappointment in this man made her long to speak her mind, but instinct warned her to keep her mouth shut.

Nor did Justin's next words do anything to appease her frame of mind. 'Do I see disapproval in your expression? Believe me—Rex is too busy with his memoirs to worry about the orchard. He must decide what to put in and what to omit.'

'You mean about the daughter who—who deserted him?' she asked while avoiding his eyes and almost choking on the words.

'Oh, I doubt that she'll even get a mention.'

'You mean, he's still filled with bitterness?'

'It's more than possible. People like Rex don't change. If you'll take my advice you won't let him know you've ever heard of her.'

'You're worried he'll know you've mentioned her?'

'*Worried*? Not in the least. It's just that I don't want him to hit the ceiling and descend in a shower of small pieces.'

Mary stood up abruptly. She remained silent as she placed the empty coffee-mugs on the tray and carried them back to the kitchen. Anger simmered within her, but she warned herself it must not be allowed to come to the boil.

Nor did it abate until they were driving along the Wainui Road towards Gisborne, which was less than four miles away, and as she sat beside Justin her spirits began to rise. Gradually her previous wrath evaporated until she became conscious of an unusual feeling of contentment which began to steal over her.

It had nothing to do with this devastating man whose hands looked so strong as they rested lightly on the steering-wheel, she assured herself. It was just the relief of being away from the sadness, and the depressing atmosphere of the house where dear old Gran's precious belongings were being sorted and packed. Yes—that was it.

CHAPTER THREE

JUSTIN made a left-hand turn which took them towards the rounded landmark of Kaiti Hill, and within a short time the road ascended steeply until it reached the summit, where it levelled to give parking area for cars. He opened the door for Mary, then led her to a look-out where they stood gazing down upon waterways and thousands of roof-tops.

'Gisborne is divided by three rivers,' he said. 'It's a city of bridges.'

She made no reply. His hand had remained on her arm, making her vitally conscious of his touch, though heaven alone knew why it should affect her. Should she shake it off? she wondered. To do so seemed churlish and meant making a fuss about nothing, therefore she allowed it to remain while her eyes wandered beyond the spread of flat land which nestled beside the foothills of a mountain range.

Pressure from Justin's hand caused her to turn and face in the opposite direction, where the panorama had changed to one of blue sea, golden beaches and lush green farmlands.

He pointed across the bay to where a headland of stark white cliffs rose out of the sea. 'There it is,' he said. 'Young Nick's Head. Or did you really expect to see somebody's head preserved in a pot?' He turned to grin at her.

'Of course not,' she defended. 'I didn't know what to think.'

He went on to explain. 'When Captain James Cook was approaching these shores back in October 1769 he noticed signs of nearby land—such things as floating seaweed, driftwood and different birds. He then promised a gallon of rum to the one who should first see land. It was Nicholas Young, the surgeon's boy, who spotted it from the masthead, therefore Cook named it Young Nick's Head. However, I doubt that the lad saw much of the rum.'

His hands slid down her arm to clasp her fingers, and again she wondered why she didn't snatch it away. Instead she allowed him to draw her towards a life-size bronze statue erected on a pedestal.

He spoke with his lips close to her ear. 'Meet the man himself. Captain James Cook, explorer extraordinary. A monument at the foot of this hill marks the place where he first stepped ashore.'

Mary looked up to examine the hand resting on the sword and the detailed sculpture of the naval uniform. And then she heard herself being introduced to the statue.

'Good morning, Captain,' Justin said with a polite bow. 'This is Miss Mary Kendall, newly arrived from that other lump of land you found across the Tasman. But instead of coming immediately to say "ahoy, there"—to a fine sailor like yourself—she went hiking off in search of citrus orchards.' He paused before asking softly, 'I wonder why?'

Mary caught his mood. She curtsied to the statue as she said, 'Pray forgive me, kind sir—I didn't know you were here waiting so patiently on your pedestal.' Then her tone changed as she turned to Justin. 'But that's not the only reason.'

'No? Enlighten me. I'm becoming interested.'

'Are you, indeed? Then hear this. Citrus orchards are alive with birds and bees. They have fruit and flowers at the same time. The air is full of perfume and the chatter of the people working there—whereas this man is in no hurry to receive my homage.'

'A happy lot, are they—the people of the orchard?'

'Well—all except the overseer, who, for some reason, is a sour fellow and full of suspicion——' She stopped, appalled by the manner in which her tongue had run away with itself, then flicked a swift glance at him while wondering if he'd taken offence.

But this did not appear to be so because he merely turned and looked towards the south. 'The Valencia is about ten miles in that direction,' he remarked.

She looked at him anxiously. 'Valencia—don't you think it's time we were moving towards it?'

He glanced at his watch then shrugged. 'OK—if you're so keen to be there. Or are you hinting I'm boring you with all this viewing?'

'No—no, of course not,' she assured him hastily. 'It's just that I'm afraid the boss—I—I mean Mr Todd—might be annoyed with you for being away from the job for so long.'

He grinned but said nothing.

They returned to the car, and as she settled herself in the comfortable grey Holden Commodore she recalled that she had expected to be collected in the utility truck she had previously seen laden with oranges for the Boy Scouts. No doubt this vehicle belonged to her grand— to Mr Todd, she decided, feeling sure he had requested Justin to use it rather than the small truck.

Moments later they were descending the hill, and after crossing bridges and driving along streets they reached the city's higher outskirts where the Gisborne Hospital was situated. The oranges and lemons were delivered, and Mary felt a sense of relief as they made their way towards the Valencia. Strangely, she had no wish to see any form of wrath fall upon Justin's head. It had been kind of him to take her up Kaiti Hill—which was something her parents had been too busy to even think about.

However, there were no black looks when they reached the Valencia homestead. Justin stopped the car at the front door, where they were greeted by a smiling Laura, who asked him to carry Mary's suitcase into the end guest-room. They then followed him along the passage to a pleasant room with its own en-suite bathroom and veranda door.

Laura spoke to Justin. 'Rex is waiting for you to pour him a pre-lunch drink, and Ella is waiting to serve lunch.'

A shade of impatience crossed his face. 'Why on earth must they insist upon waiting for me? I've told Rex to help himself.'

As he left the room Mary turned to Laura, her expression apologetic. 'I'm sorry if we're late. It's really my fault because the moment I admitted I hadn't been up Kaiti Hill Justin decided I should see the view.'

Laura laughed. 'Don't blame yourself for his decisions. He's a man who makes his own rules.'

Mary looked at her uncertainly, not at all sure of her meaning. It seemed an odd remark to make, and in an effort to explain herself further she said, 'I wouldn't like to think I'd caused trouble for him with the boss.'

It was Laura's turn to look puzzled. 'The *boss*? You mean *Rex*—my husband?'

'Yes. It was kind of Mr Todd to allow him to collect me in his nice Holden. It appears to be quite a new car.'

Laura smiled. 'My dear, you've been jumping to wrong conclusions, but I suppose it's only natural because you can't possibly know the situation here. To begin with, that Holden Commodore belongs to Justin, while Rex is content to drive the old Ford he's had for umpteen years.'

'Oh.' Mary fell silent, waiting to hear more.

Laura went on, 'As for the matter of who is the boss round these parts—well, that happens to be Justin.'

Mary controlled the shock that almost caused her jaw to sag. '*Justin*? But I thought...' The words dwindled to nothing.

'You thought Rex owned the place? Those days are over. He owned it for many years until he reached the stage of deciding to retire. In fact he'd made up his mind to sell the property when Justin came to stay with us.'

'And—he bought it?' The question was little more than a whisper as Mary began to realise how mistaken she had been.

'That's right. He was able to do so because a bachelor uncle had made him his heir. However, he had no desire to live here alone or with strangers, so he persuaded Rex to continue living in the house and to become his overseer—but only when he felt like it.'

Mary had an insane desire to shriek with laughter. Laura was right in saying she'd been jumping to conclusions, but how could she do otherwise than assume that the situation was the one that had become settled in her mind?

But now she knew that the reverse was the case. Justin was the boss—her grandfather was the overseer when he felt like stretching his legs in the orchard. To Mary it was ludicrous until she thought about it and realised that this was Justin's way of allowing the old man to retain the authority he'd enjoyed for so long.

At last she took a deep breath and said calmly, 'It sounds like a very good arrangement.'

'Excellent,' Laura agreed. 'Rex had no real desire to leave the place he'd lived in for so long, and he has really enjoyed teaching Justin the routine of citrus orchard management. Everything has gone on as before, except that the responsibility of the place has slid from older to younger shoulders.'

'Justin appears to be very—benevolent,' Mary said, recalling the load of oranges donated to the Scouts, and the amount of fruit left at the hospital.

'Yes. Rex declares him to be generous to a fault. It is not surprising that people refer to him as the orchard king,' Laura added with a smile.

'The orchard king,' Mary repeated thoughtfully. 'At least it's most appropriate. They're the best oranges I've ever tasted.'

'So they should be after all the expensive fertiliser he's piled round the trees,' Laura responded briskly. 'Now then, I'd better see if Ella needs help in serving lunch. She's my companion-help without whose assistance I'd be unable to run this house. When you're ready you'll find the dining-room at the other end of the passage.'

But instead of being in a hurry to leave the bedroom Mary paused to ponder this new piece of information. So her grandfather had not only remarried—he no longer owned the orchard. It belonged to Justin, who must have sensed she had taken him to be one of the staff. But not a word had he said, and his tolerant acceptance of her error made her suspect he regarded her as being thoroughly stupid.

The thought riled her, making her feel reluctant to face him again, but she knew it had to be done; therefore to give herself extra confidence she hastily applied more make-up and gave rapid brush-strokes to her dark hair. The blue eyes that stared back at her from the mirror betrayed her disinclination to venture forth, but at last she took a grip on her courage and stepped out into the passage.

Justin was waiting for her. Leaning nonchalantly against a doorway, he drawled, 'I thought you'd never emerge.'

She was startled. 'I didn't realise you'd be waiting for me.'

'Let's say I've come to make sure you find your way to the dining-room. After all, you're in a strange house.'

'You think I'd have difficulty, with that appetising aroma wafting along the passage?'

'Not really.' He chuckled then admitted, 'Actually it was Rex who feared you might get lost by wandering out to the packing shed via the side door. He's keen to greet you. It's almost as if he's bursting to have another look at you.' The last words came flippantly.

She felt a sudden apprehension. 'Oh? Why would that be?'

'He thinks you remind him of somebody.'

Mary brushed the suggestion aside with a light laugh. 'No doubt I'm like one of the pickers who has worked in the orchard at some time. I think you'll find that his real anxiety lies in the desire to see me at the typewriter.'

'It's possible.' He frowned, then paused outside the dining-room door to mutter in a low voice, 'I should warn you that he can be a tough nut to work for. He'll keep you at it till your eyes strike fire, and they'll do just that while you're trying to decipher his atrocious handwriting.'

When they entered the room Rex Todd rose to his feet. He bent a long and penetrating stare upon Mary, but before he could speak Laura came from the kitchen. She was followed by a small, slightly built middle-aged woman who pushed an oak trolley laden with plates and a casserole of vegetables resting beside a fish pie.

Laura made the introduction. 'Miss Kendall—this is Mrs Mills, although I'm sure she'd prefer to be called Ella.'

Mary went to Ella and offered her hand. 'And I prefer to be called Mary,' she said with a smile that seemed to light her face.

Rex's eyes were on Mary's wavy hair as he asked, 'Would you care for a sherry before your lunch?'

She glanced at the large crystal jug occupying the centre of the dining table. 'No, thank you—although the contents of that jug look inviting.'

Ella beamed. 'That's my own special brew of orangeade.' She moved to the table and filled a small glass, which she handed to Mary. 'If you like it you can have the recipe.'

One sip was sufficient to make Mary say, 'It's delicious. Thank you—I'd love to have the recipe.'

Justin spoke to Mary, his tone amused. 'You may consider yourself to be honoured. Ella favours very few people with her secrets—or so I've been given to understand by one person who has made several requests for that particular recipe.'

Ella's expression became defiant. 'I don't give my recipes to people who tell me to my face that I should be eating in the kitchen instead of in the dining-room— or that I should at least be placed below the salt, like a menial, at the master's table.'

Justin scowled. 'Come off it, Ella. You're exaggerating. Those days are well in the past. They've completely disappeared.'

'Not for some people, they haven't,' she retorted sharply.

'Is it possible you're accusing Rochelle of treating you in this manner?' he drawled.

'Who else?' Ella queried calmly, then looked at Laura. 'Would you like me to serve for you?'

'Of course—thank you, Ella. Now then, Mary, you'll sit here—and we'll see if we can find something more pleasant to discuss.' Laura's tone had become firm.

But Justin had not quite finished with that subject, and, sending a teasing glance towards Ella, he pursued, 'What makes you so sure Mary doesn't hold similar views to Rochelle?'

Ella gave a short laugh. 'Her friendly smile and firm handshake spoke for themselves.' She sent him a direct look. 'I may not have the education of some people, but I'm not entirely dim-witted. I reckon I know quality when I see it.'

Mary looked down at the delicious fish pie with chips and peas on her plate. 'I'm beginning to feel embarrassed,' she admitted.

Rex, who had said very little since she had entered the room, now spoke drily. 'At least you have won Ella's approval, and that can't be said of everyone round these parts. Rochelle, for instance, is well down the ladder, though only the devil knows why. She's a good-looking girl who will inherit a fine piece of land that's been well planted——' He broke off to shoot a significant look at Justin.

'That's enough of that claptrap, you scheming old buzzard.' Justin grinned to soften the words.

Rex scowled at him. 'I'm thinking of your own good.'

Justin's lips thinned. 'Rubbish. You just want to see the orchard expand. It'd help your own ego no end.'

Laura spoke sharply. 'Now stop it, you two. Remember we have a guest.' She turned to Mary. 'They're really very fond of each other, so take no notice of anything that sounds—untoward.'

After that the conversation switched to matters concerning the orchard, and while Mary listened with interest her mind continued to hover round the question of Rochelle who lived on the neighbouring property. Was she the daughter of the man Mother had been expected to marry? Was history repeating itself?

Surreptitiously she examined the weather-beaten lines on the older man's face, knowing they indicated years of outdoor work. Nor was it difficult to guess that he could see yet another opportunity for his beloved orchard to become united with the one next door. And even if he no longer owned it, he would not have hesitated to make his hopes clear to Justin.

But what were Justin's feeling towards Rochelle? she wondered. He had already indicated he considered she should be typing the memoirs—in fact given another chance after her first failure. Did this mean she was never far from his thoughts? Well—so what? His emotional life was not a matter that concerned herself.

And then she became aware of the darting glances coming from beneath her grandfather's shaggy grey brows. Despite the fact that he appeared to be taking part in a discussion concerning the packing shed, his eyes were covertly observing the movement of her hands and the manner in which she used her fork. It was almost as though memory was causing him to make comparisons—nor was it difficult to guess with whom.

To divert his attention from her appearance she asked, 'Where would you like me to work?'

'In the office,' he replied without hesitation.

The office? her mind queried while trying to recall her mother's description of the house. Then she guessed it would be the room referred to as the study. 'I always did my school homework in the study,' Elizabeth had told her. 'It was such a cosy little room with an open fireplace and lined with Father's books. It also had a door opening out to a covered walk leading to the packing shed, and staff came to it to collect their wages.'

Rex's voice cut into her thoughts. 'Justin will share the office with you at times, but I doubt that he'll disturb you.'

'Because his mind will be on somebody else?' Mary smiled teasingly, then wondered what had prompted her to make such a remark.

Nor did an answering smile come from Justin. 'The lady's imagination is running away with her,' he informed the others blandly. 'She does not understand that my mind will be occupied by such matters as sprays and fertilisers.'

Mary sensed the gentle snub behind his words, but she ignored it by saying, 'I presume there's a routine plan for applying these things? Certain times and so forth?'

'Of course. The fertilising programme is split into three applications during October, December and February, but the spraying programme stretches from October to the following June because not all citrus trees bloom at the same time.' He paused while looking at her thoughtfully before adding, 'Or do these mundane facts bore you to tears?'

'Not at all,' she retorted crisply. 'I've already told you of my interest in learning about citrus orchards.'

'So you have,' he commented in a tone that was full of mockery while his eyes flashed a look of enquiry at Rex and Laura. 'Can either of you imagine why?'

Rex frowned. 'Why shouldn't Mary wish to learn about a citrus orchard?' he queried gruffly. 'She could be really interested——'

'I'm sure she is,' Justin replied blandly. 'It's just that I'm curious to know *why*.' His eyes were full of questions as they gazed steadily at Mary.

She knew that his mind was loaded with doubts concerning herself—doubts that caused him to wonder why she was there, and as she glared at him across the table she said in a cool voice, 'It seems to please you to regard me as an interloper.'

Rex leaned forward and patted her hand. 'Take no notice of him, my dear. He's jealous because you'll be working for me.'

Justin chuckled. 'A fact which will be used as an excuse to remain indoors to breathe down Mary's neck.'

Rex was affronted by the suggestion. 'I'll merely show her what has to be done and let her get on with it,' he declared stiffly.

Mary knew an inner relief. Justin's hint that her grandfather might haunt the office was something that she herself had feared, and now that it had been swept away—at least to a certain extent—she was suddenly anxious to get on with the job. Turning to Rex, she asked quietly, 'Isn't it time I made a start?'

Approval flashed from the blue eyes. 'If you've finished your lunch we'll go to the office.' Then he pushed his chair back.

They left the room, and although Mary felt Justin's eyes following her she did not look back at him. He was a disturbing man, she decided, and she had no intentions of allowing thoughts of him to interfere with the work lying ahead—especially with *his* mind hovering round Rochelle. What was she like, this Rochelle?

When they reached the office she was amazed by the accuracy of her mother's description, although she could see that additions had been made because there were now two desks instead of one. And there was something else that Mother had never mentioned—a large portrait that hung above the mantelpiece.

It was of a woman dressed in blue—a woman whose likeness to herself gave her a shock. An invisible magnet drew her closer to stand and stare up at the dark hair and creamy complexion, and at her own eyes that gazed back at her. 'Who is that?' she asked at last, her voice coming as little more than a whisper.

'That's Mary, my first wife,' he said in a tone that had softened to the extent of not sounding at all like him.

'She—she's very attractive,' Mary said, feeling that something of a complimentary nature was expected of her.

'You're surprisingly like her. I noticed it the moment I set eyes on you,' he admitted.

Mary could find nothing to say while wondering why her mother had never mentioned the portrait. It couldn't possibly be something she'd forget, she thought while trying to place a date on the style of dress, and at last she asked, 'When was it done?'

'Before I married Laura,' he said gruffly. 'There was a period when I was alone in this house. It was most depressing and I longed to have Mary to talk to. But she wasn't here because she'd died years previously. Then I had the idea of having a photo blown up and a portrait in oils painted from it. I must say the artist fellow made a darned good job of it.'

So this was something else that Mother didn't know about, Mary thought, realising that the portrait had been painted after she'd left. Then, deciding it was time to get off the subject, she turned to the pile of papers sitting beside the portable typewriter. In fact there were more papers than she had expected to see, although she gave no hint of this as she lifted a page covered by the elderly man's handwriting.

'Can you read it?' he asked, watching her anxiously.

'Parts of it are clear—while parts are difficult,' she said after frowning over it for a short time. However, the fact that it had a strange similarity to her mother's writing seemed to lessen the difficulty.

He shuffled and sorted pages, then said, 'Perhaps you could make a start from here?'

She settled herself on the chair, placed carbon paper between two sheets of blank paper and inserted them into the machine. 'It's like beginning a story in the middle,' she said, sending him a brief smile before setting her fingers to work.

He watched her for several minutes before he exclaimed, 'Good grief—you can type without looking at the keys!'

'It's called touch-typing,' she explained.

He hesitated then said, 'Perhaps the first chapters should be retyped. They're a mass of corrections. Here they are.'

She nodded, feeling a glow of satisfaction as he placed them beside her. Already she'd been wondering how she could read the first chapters without appearing to be too inquisitive about their contents. Nor had she any wish for him to come into the room unexpectedly and discover her perusing them.

He left the room and she worked steadily until three-thirty when Ella brought her a cup of tea and fingers of sweet crisp shortbread. By that time several pages had been deciphered and typed, and as the small woman looked at them she exclaimed, 'My goodness—that lot looks different! The poor man was having a real struggle—what with peering at the dictionary and hitting the keys with one finger——' She broke off abruptly to stare through the window then exclaimed, 'There she is— that's Rochelle!'

Mary tried to remain uninterested, but curiosity caused her to leave the typewriter and join Ella at the window. To the right of the packing-shed path was a small patch of lawn surrounded by a tree-sheltered garden. However, it was not the spring flowers that caught and held Mary's attention, it was Justin and the woman who stood beside him—a woman whose blonde beauty was not to be denied.

'Are they old friends?' Mary probed while looking at the long fair tresses that swung below the silken-clad shoulders.

'Not really. When Justin first came here she was living in England, but a couple of years ago she came home after a broken marriage. One look at *him* was enough to make her set her cap at him, and when she comes visiting she always manages to entice him out to that quiet spot,' Ella added darkly.

Or does Justin entice Rochelle towards its seclusion? Mary wondered, watching as Rochelle stooped to pluck a large pansy, brush it across her lips, then place it in the pocket of Justin's shirt.

Ella drew a sharp breath. 'There now—I *told* you she's doing her best to pin him down. Pansies for *thoughts*, you understand.'

'One must admit she's rather lovely,' Mary said generously, noting the perfection of Rochelle's slim form.

'Only on the outside,' Ella sniffed cynically. 'I'm hoping he'll have the sense to see it before he's caught up in those bleached strands hanging down her back.'

Mary's eyes widened. 'Bleached? All that hair?'

'Of course. She's far too dark near the scalp for that flaxen mass to be natural,' Ella pointed out scornfully. 'But, as she's rising towards thirty, I suppose she must make the best of herself.' Ella looked at Mary significantly as she added, 'And because she lives next door she's trying to establish an affinity with Justin—a sort of prior claim based on mutual orchard interests.'

Mary looked at her thoughtfully. 'Aren't you forgetting Justin's side of this friendship? He might also sense there's an—an affinity. Don't most men find blondes attractive?'

'Some men, perhaps,' Ella sniffed. 'But I wouldn't have thought that a man such as Justin could be taken in by the likes of *her*.'

'She could be really in love,' Mary suggested.

'She sure is,' Ella agreed. 'With herself. Well, I'll leave you to finish your tea. Be in the living-room by six o'clock, when we have a drink while watching the TV news.'

'I'll be there,' Mary promised. Would Rochelle also be there? she wondered.

'After the news I serve dinner,' Ella said from the doorway. 'It's early by the standards of some people, but this is a household where we're early to bed and early to rise.'

Mary continued to sip her tea, her eyes watching Justin and Rochelle from across the rim of her cup. They were close enough for her to see the blonde smiling winningly while gazing up into his face, and she could also see that his expression had remained serious, almost as if failing to respond to Rochelle's vivacious chatter.

And then he turned towards the house and caught her in the act of observing them through the office window. She drew back hastily, embarrassed by being discovered in what appeared to be an exercise of spying, and as she saw him make strides towards the house she gulped the remains of her tea and hastened to settle herself before the typewriter.

When the door opened he was followed by Rochelle, and as he made the introduction his voice held a hint of amusement. 'Rochelle Grover—Mary Kendall.'

Mary found herself looking into pale grey eyes that glinted with a sparkle of ice. They were rimmed with heavy mascara, and for once she was thankful for her own long dark lashes.

Justin explained, 'Mary has offered to help old Rex out of his typing mess.'

'I'll bet she has.' Rochelle's lips thinned as she made a cool appraisal of Mary's features, then she pouted at Justin. 'Why didn't you arrange for me to do it?'

His brows rose in surprise. 'Are you forgetting you've already made one attempt? Rex could hardly contain his irritation, if I remember correctly.'

'That was because you didn't stay near to help me decipher his awful scrawl,' she complained, looking at him reproachfully.

'Would you have had me neglect my work?'

'Of course not—but Justin, *dear*, you could have sent him out to the orchard instead of allowing him to hang round the office. After all, you are the *boss*, and—and it would've been so *nice* to—to work on it *together*,' she added naïvely.

Justin gave a sigh of infinite patience as he explained, 'Things don't work in that manner round these parts. I do not order Rex to toil in the orchard. He knows exactly what has to be done and he pleases himself as to whether or not he does it. The man has now retired—you understand?'

Rochelle's mouth became sulky. 'I—I suppose so.'

He went on, 'I'll leave you two girls to get to know each other. If you'll excuse me I have matters to attend to in the packing shed.'

Rochelle waited until he'd closed the door behind him, then her eyes went to the portrait above the mantelpiece. 'Who are you?' she demanded abruptly. 'Are you a relative of some sort?'

'What on earth makes you think so?' Mary hedged.

'Your likeness to *her*, of course. You even do your hair in that outmoded manner.'

Mary sat very straight in her chair as she looked directly at Rochelle. 'Are you always so rude to people you've only just met?'

'Only if they're likely to trespass on to my preserve,' Rochelle informed her loftily.

Mary forced a blank expression on to her face. 'Your preserve—what would that be?'

'My territory, of course.'

'Oh—I see—you mean this typing job?'

'Of course not,' Rochelle sneered. 'You're more than welcome to *that*. My oath—if you don't know what I'm getting at you must be mighty dumb.' She paused to consider Mary reflectively, her eyes returning to the portrait as she said, 'Eyes—nose—mouth—you've even got her dimple. And that reminds me, you didn't answer my question. Are you a relative?'

Mary's shoulders lifted in a faint shrug. 'How could I be? I'm newly arrived from Australia.'

'*Australia*?' Rochelle's pale eyes narrowed slightly but she said nothing further.

However, Mary was left with the uncomfortable feeling that she should not have made that admission, and then she reminded herself that as the rest of the household already knew this fact it was of little importance. Yet somehow she felt she'd made a mistake.

This seemed to be proved by Rochelle's next words. 'Old Rex had a relative who went to Aussie,' the blonde mused thoughtfully. 'I was only a child at the time but I remember there was a fuss of some sort. I must ask my parents about it. They'll remember.'

Mary's heart sank. It was as though an enquiry concerning her identity had started already. She turned to the typewriter with what she hoped was a gesture of dismissal, and, ignoring Rochelle, she began to concentrate upon deciphering a page of difficult scrawl.

Rochelle watched her for several moments before she said in a sharp tone, 'I hope you'll remember what I said.'

Mary sent a smile over her shoulder. 'I'm afraid I'm too busy to remember anything you've said.'

As she spoke the door leading outside opened to admit Justin. He was in time to hear Mary's words, and looking from one to the other he queried, 'What is Mary too busy to remember?'

Rochelle spoke rapidly. 'Only my questions about herself,' she lied. 'Since my return to New Zealand I'm finding myself to be interested in everyone I meet. It's so different from the large cities overseas where people are uncaring about others.'

'Really?' Justin sounded amused. 'Are you saying you've developed a special interest in Mary?'

'Her likeness to that portrait intrigues me. I can't help wondering if she's a relative—especially as she comes from *Australia*,' she added with a degree of innocence.

Justin frowned. 'I can guess your trend of thought, but don't you realise that Mary bears a name that's different from the one you have in mind?'

'Well—I find it difficult to get over the likeness,' Rochelle persisted stubbornly. 'Hasn't anyone else in the house noticed it?'

'Oh, yes—we're all aware of it,' Justin drawled.

Rochelle ignored Mary's presence as she went on, 'In that case you'll have realised there must be a reason for one with such strong family resemblances to have arrived at this place—*such as an inheritance*——'

Justin's eyes became hooded as he said, 'Mary assured me she was just looking, thanks.'

Rochelle spoke sneeringly. 'And she liked what she saw—therefore she decided to ingratiate herself with the old man. I'm very surprised that you can't see *that* for yourself, Justin.'

Suppressed anger caused Mary to break into their conversation. Frostily, she said, 'Fascinating as I find this discussion concerning myself, I'd be grateful if it could be carried on elsewhere. It is interrupting my work—and it is not one that amuses me.'

Justin stared at her in silence, his eyes thoughtful as they moved from her face to the one in the portrait. Then he spoke crisply to Rochelle. 'You said you want to see fruit picked from trees near our mutual boundary. There are some in the packing shed, but I'm sure you'll find there's very little difference from your own.'

Rochelle smiled winningly. 'Mother declares that your oranges are larger than ours. If so, I want to know what fertiliser you use.'

He laughed. 'You're so sure I'll tell you my secrets?'

She sent him a look of wide-eyed appeal. 'I—I thought it might be possible. Isn't it Rex's dream that these two orchards should be run as one unit—some day?' she added coyly.

'Rex dreams too much,' Justin retorted tersely. 'It's time he woke up.' He sent a cool glance towards Mary, one that was filled with suspicion as he muttered, 'OK, we'll leave you to get on with it.'

Rochelle also regarded her icily, her eyes holding unveiled hostility that warned Mary she had an enemy.

CHAPTER FOUR

MARY remained perfectly still after the door had closed, then, when several long moments had passed, she raised her eyes to the portrait. 'Are you about to betray me, Grandmother?' she whispered. 'You know, I didn't count on your presence in this place.'

The luminous blue eyes stared back at her, and while the lips were unable to speak their message seemed to come through clearly. Get out—before you're thrown out.

But these memoirs—I must do them, Mary's mind argued.

The answer that came was contradictory. Then get on with them. Don't just sit there gawping at me.

And as the advice seeped into Mary's brain she turned once more to the papers on the desk. In any case, what excuse could she find for giving up so soon? Nor did she wish to find herself being branded as one who had said she would take on a task, and had then reneged. It was like breaking a promise.

It would also lower her in Justin's eyes. Are you one who goes back on your word? he had queried yesterday when walking in the orchard. The memory of his words now made her realise she was caught in a trap of her own making.

The thought of Justin sent her mind along a track where concentration was difficult. His face hovered a few inches above the typewriter, and she kept waiting for the sound of his steps on the path outside the door. But he was with Rochelle, she reminded herself, and therefore unlikely to return to the office.

This was just as well, Mary felt certain. He was a disturbing man, capable of disrupting not only her work, but also herself—personally. And this was something she had no intention of allowing, because dreaming of *him* would get her precisely nowhere. Hadn't he said he preferred to remain free of the female species? 'OK, Your Majesty—I've got the message,' she muttered in a low voice.

The thought enabled her to brush him from her mind, and as her concentration became more intense the minutes passed rapidly. Indeed the time flew so quickly that she did not realise the hour until Justin spoke from behind her.

'Didn't you hear the chimes from the hall clock? It's past five.'

She turned to stare at him. 'Is it? So what?'

'So it's time you came out for a breath of fresh air. You've worked long enough for one afternoon.'

'Are you putting me on set hours?'

'No—but I'm taking you away from that typewriter.'

'Isn't that rather high-handed on your part? Aren't I working for Mr Todd? Shouldn't he be the one to tell me when to stop?'

Justin laughed. 'You'll wait a long time for him to tell you to call it a day. He's reading the paper with a glass of Scotch in his hand. I've told him you're finished for today.'

'Oh?' In truth she was ready to leave the work, but not because Justin had decreed she should do so, therefore she sent him a glare of defiance as she said, 'Your Majesty might have royal prerogative where members of your orchard staff are concerned, but it does not apply to me.'

His annoyance was apparent. 'You can cut out that silly orchard king nonsense.'

A mocking laugh escaped her. 'Don't tell me it doesn't do a little something for your ego.'

'Nothing at all. Nor do I know how it began,' he snapped.

'I've been told it's from your own name and the excellent oranges you grow in your orchard—Mr King. I presume that a special fertiliser of some sort is the name of the game. Have you a secret formula?'

He scowled. 'You've been listening to Ella's flow of humbug.'

'Ella? No, I haven't.'

'She'll tell you that some people imagine I've worked out a special formula for growing particularly good oranges.'

'And have you been successful? Is this what Rochelle is so anxious to learn?'

'I'll admit I've experimented, but the results are always the same. I think it's mainly that we're fortunate in having the type of soil and conditions that oranges need. They're the least hardy of the citrus fruits but ours are sheltered by the she-oaks and the Gisborne climate is kind to them. So, having exploded the myth of a secret formula, shall we take a stroll in the fresh air?'

Again she hesitated without quite knowing why, apart from the fact that she realised that this man was having an effect upon her. The magnetism of his male aura reached out to engulf her, and, shrinking back mentally, she asked, 'Haven't you had sufficient fresh air for one day? You've been outside for hours.'

'Yes—but you haven't.'

'I took in plenty up on Kaiti Hill,' she argued. 'What's more it was laden with the tang of the sea.'

'Nevertheless you'll come for a walk to stretch your legs,' he declared in a firm tone, then opened the door to lead her down the steps towards the secluded garden.

She went without further protest, conscious of the fact that her obvious reluctance had been somewhat ungracious, yet knowing that it stemmed from the thought that he probably guided all his female visitors towards its hidden corners.

From the office door she had been unable to see into
the main area of the garden, but now, as they turned
the corner, she was faced by beauty that caused her to
catch her breath. Hardly a leaf stirred in the early evening
stillness where flowering cherry trees stretched blossom-
laden branches above the brilliant reds, yellows, oranges
and pinks of azaleas. Below them were blue grape
hyacinths.

'It's all so lovely,' she murmured. 'I had no idea such
colour lay so close to where I sat typing.'

'I wanted to make sure you saw it at its best,' he said
quietly. 'A heavy downpour of rain will rob it of perfection.' He paused, then regarded her with a suspicion
of amusement. 'Incidentally, Rex was curious to learn
where I'd found you.'

'Really?' She avoided his eyes by bending to breathe
the heady aroma of a purple Australian mint bush. 'So
what did you tell him?'

'The truth, of course. I said I'd found you wandering
like a lost soul in the orchard.'

'Which made him wonder if I'd sneaked in to steal
fruit, I suppose—just as you yourself thought——'

'I told him you have a special fondness for oranges—
and perhaps a special interest in meeting the people who
grow them. Would that be correct?'

She was unsure whether the question was loaded with
amusement or suspicion. Did he suspect her identity?
Or did this highly eligible man have the utter *temerity*
to imagine she had heard about *him* and had come with
the purpose of meeting him? She'd soon put him right
on that score, she decided, and, controlling the irritation building within herself, she spoke loftily.

'What makes you think I'm crazy about *oranges*—or
anyone even remotely connected with them? To be honest
I much prefer tangelos—like large reddish-orange mandarins. Their flesh is so sweet and juicy, and their seg-
ments are pulled apart so easily.'

He sent her a sharp glance. 'Is it possible you like to see things pulled apart?'

The question jolted her, causing her to stand still while she stared at him. 'What on earth would put such a thought into your head?' she demanded indignantly.

He regarded her steadily. 'Just the fact that some people have an urge to destroy. They like to pull others apart.'

Her chin rose. 'Do you suspect I'm here to pull anyone apart? If so, I consider your remarks to be insulting.'

'Simmer down,' he soothed, then unexpectedly took her hand to draw her towards a path leading away from the garden.

His action startled her, causing her to draw back, then she told herself not to be stupid. He was merely making amends for his previous remarks, and was quite unaware that his touch almost sent a shock up her arm.

'You're still taking umbrage?' he queried, sending her a quizzical glance from eyes that again held amusement.

She thought rapidly then lied, 'Not at all. I was taking a last look at the glorious colours of the azaleas.'

His grip tightened on her fingers, almost as if he expected her to snatch her hand away, yet his tone remained casual as he said, 'Ella has a book which gives the meanings of flowers. Only this morning she told me that azaleas indicate temperance, and that the polyanthus primrose means confidence.'

'And pansies are for loving thoughts,' she said, forcing a smile as she admitted, 'I saw Rochelle put one in your shirt pocket. I presume it's still there?'

'I dare say it is,' he responded nonchalantly.

'Then why are you holding hands with me?' she demanded sharply, and instantly pulled her fingers free of his clasp.

The path had taken them between the cherry trees, and, standing still, he looked at her with undisguised surprise.

Contritely, she said, 'I'm sorry—it's not my concern if every pocket you possess is stuffed with flowers from Rochelle.' Then, to cover her embarrassment, she turned to pluck a sprig of delicate blossoms from a low branch.

But the sprig did not come away easily, and her efforts to remove it brought down a shower of fluttering blossoms. They rested upon her dark hair and shoulders, and as Justin paused to remove them his expression became serious.

Puzzled, she looked up at him then asked, 'Is something wrong? What do cherry blossoms mean in Ella's book?'

His mouth became grim while his silence continued.

She became aware of an inner concern. 'Tell me—what do they mean?' She waited apprehensively.

'Deception.' The word was snapped abruptly.

She was amazed. 'Deception? Surely there's a mistake. How could those lovely pink and white clusters of blossoms mean anything quite so unpleasant?'

'Possibly because they appear to be a symbol of happiness that will go on forever. Instead their life is so short that they've gone before happiness can make itself really felt.' He fell silent, staring at her intently, then remarked in a strangely thoughtful voice, 'I trust that these petals still clinging to you are not offering me a warning.'

Her eyes were widened slightly. 'I don't understand what you mean. A warning against what?'

His dark brows drew together. 'I'm not sure. I'll admit you've got me puzzled—nor am I at all happy about the reason you've given for being in the orchard.'

She laughed. 'Are you telling me you really believe in this folklore? I can hardly credit——'

'Of course I don't take it as gospel. But one's mind is apt to reach in all directions when seeking the answer to a question that keeps nagging,' he admitted testily.

'Why not forget it? Give the answer a chance to pop up of its own accord.' If only he would do that, she thought, it would give her time to finish the memoirs and leave the place before he became aware of her identity.

'Forget it, you say? That's easier said than done. I could wipe it off my mind if you'd been the average orchard wanderer who snatches a bag of fruit and disappears. But you're not. Something about you goes deeper than that.'

'Like what?'

'Like the fact that you've now wangled your way into the house. In an incredibly short time you've become like one of the family. Hell's teeth—you even *look* like one of the family. You'll recall I said I thought I'd seen you before? The reason for that hangs over the office mantelpiece.'

She shrugged. 'So we're look-alikes.'

'To the extent that you've got old Rex intrigued—especially as you've arrived out of the blue.'

'There's something unusual about that?'

'Definitely—where he's concerned. He's inclined to be somewhat sour where girls of your age are involved.'

'And that makes you fear there's something *deceptive* about me?' Staring up at him, she awaited his answer while a sudden fear gnawed at her mind. Had he guessed at the true reason for her interest in the orchard, and for her offer to type Rex Todd's memoirs? Was he playing her along like a tomcat with a mouse?

And then another thought struck her. Was it an act of deceit to keep her mother's identity hidden from him? She told herself it was not—and that it was her own private concern—and even as she pondered the question he bent his head swiftly and kissed her on the mouth.

The action drew a gasp from her, causing her to step back rapidly. Blue sparks flashed in her eyes as she demanded coldly, 'Who gave you permission to do that?'

He grinned. 'You did. I saw it written on your own lips. They looked so inviting, I was unable to resist the impulse.'

She took a deep breath. 'That's what I call a colossal nerve—to say nothing of an outsized imagination.'

'Didn't you know that the human race is governed by its own imagination? It's imagination that gets us places.'

'Are you trying to excuse yourself by uttering platitudes?'

'Not at all. It doesn't take too much imagination to sense your need to be loved.'

She glared at him, her eyes dark with fury. 'My oath, you're an arrogant devil.'

'Yes, I sure am,' he agreed. 'Allow me to prove it.' His hands on her shoulders drew her towards him again, yet despite her mental vexation Mary made no protest.

In some intangible manner she seemed to have dissolved into the state of being hypnotised by the strength of his fingers cutting into her flesh and by the nearness of his body pressing against her breasts. In fact she actually raised her face to meet the lips that nuzzled and teased her own, then, making an effort to quench the fire that raced through her veins, she drew back and tried to control the tremor in her voice as she asked a question.

'Is this the way you kiss Rochelle?'

His voice became cool. 'Who's been telling you I've kissed her?'

She gave a small shaky laugh. 'Would I have to be told? She's rather beautiful—and she's a blonde.'

'So she's a blonde. So what? Does that give her the edge over every other girl?' He ran firm fingers through Mary's dark tresses.

'It's possible, particularly in the eyes of some men.'

'Not this one,' he said in a bored tone.

'But you *have* kissed Rochelle,' she found herself persisting in an accusing tone and without waiting to question whether or not she had the right to do so.

He sighed, then drawled nonchalantly while watching her through narrowed lids, 'Yes—I've kissed Rochelle. Does it concern you in some way?'

'Not at all,' she retorted loftily while wondering why the knowledge had the power to irritate her.

His brows rose. 'In that case, why mention the subject? What put it into your mind?'

'The cherry blossoms on your shoulders and collar,' she informed him smugly while picking them off and then displaying them in the palm of her hand. 'They mean deception, you said. Are you sure that shower of petals wasn't meant for *you* rather than for *me*?'

His mouth tightened. 'What are you driving at?'

'Perhaps they send a silent message—one that warns of *your* deception towards Rochelle while kissing me.'

'*Touché,*' he said, admitting to the point made against him, then demanded with a hint of impatience, 'What makes you imagine I owe loyalty to Rochelle? Where exactly did you get that idea?' Again his eyes had narrowed as he awaited her answer.

Mary remained silent while recalling Ella's words concerning Rochelle's ambition to 'pin him down'—however she did not dare to repeat them. At the same time, despite his scowl, she noticed no definite denial of a close association with Rochelle, therefore she decided it would be wise to change the subject. 'We're taking a long time to reach the tangelos,' she said.

'You're right. Come this way.'

The path continued towards the kitchen end of the house where it opened on to a wide backyard. As they began to cross it Mary stood still to gaze about her, noticing that the utility truck, the tractor and the cars driven by Justin and her grandfather were sheltered in various garages or sheds.

He was amused by her interest. 'Back yards have a special fascination for you?'

She avoided his eyes. 'Everything in this country interests me. It is so different from Australia, which is so vast, whereas New Zealand is—compact. One is never far from high hills.'

He continued to regard her closely. 'Is it my imagination—or do you feel a particular interest in the Valencia?' The question came casually.

'Oh, not more than in any other place,' she lied, raking in her mind for further words with which to convince him. 'Perhaps I'm intrigued by the difference between city life in Sydney and country life in New Zealand.'

'You've told me very little about your life in Sydney.'

'I can't think why you'd be interested.'

'Call it mild curiosity. I like to know about the people living under my roof, even if they are here for only a short time.'

His roof. The words jolted her into remembering that the property no longer belonged to her grandfather, and, speaking carefully, she said, 'Didn't I tell you I worked as a typist? My employer was a literary agent with an office in Chatswood until he decided to return to England.'

'There was no suggestion that you should accompany him?'

'Certainly not.' The answer came sharply. 'Why should I do that? He can find scores of typists in London.'

'I'm aware of that fact,' he retorted, then said bluntly, 'I merely wondered if there had been an emotional involvement between you. Some bosses are very close to their secretaries.'

'Not in this case,' she informed him coldly. 'He returned to England because his wife had become homesick for her own people, and because there were grandparents who were anxious to see the children. Not like one grandparent I could mention——' She stopped abruptly, appalled by the carelessness of her own runaway tongue.

He sent her an enquiring glance. 'Yes? You were about to say?'

She bit her lip. 'Well—I did hear about one grandparent who couldn't care less about the offspring of his own child.' Even that was a stupid thing to say, she chided herself, and, holding her breath, she awaited his query for more details.

But it did not come because his mind appeared to be on more personal details concerning herself. This sexy fellow who claimed a strong determination to remain fancy-free now regarded her in a quizzical manner as he probed, 'Well, if you weren't close to your recent boss, no doubt you're involved with someone?'

She shook her head as she declared firmly, 'No—no one at all,' then wondered why she was finding it necessary to assure him on this point. After all, it was not his business.

He remained silent while leading her to a secluded part of the orchard where the tangelo trees were laden with golden balls in the various stages of ripeness. 'I'm glad of that,' he said at last.

The admission surprised her. 'You are? I wonder why,' she mused while keeping her gaze fixed on the concave base of a nearby fruit. 'I mean—it can't possibly be of interest to you.'

'It just happens that I'm not in the habit of kissing girls who are attached to other fellows. You can call it a hangover from my previous experience—if you recall my mentioning it.'

She turned serious eyes upon him. 'Oh, yes—you said you'd been let down by someone to whom you were almost engaged. And, believe me, I also dislike being kissed by a man whose intentions are leaning towards somebody else.' She swallowed nervously then added, 'I trust you're getting the message and—and that there's no need to go into details or to—to mention names.'

'Yes, I've got the message,' he responded grimly. 'It's known as deceit.'

'With a capital D,' she added despite the guilty qualms growing steadily within herself.

'Naturally you're referring to deceit on my part towards Rochelle!' he exclaimed in a tone that carried amusement.

She nodded wordlessly.

He stepped closer to her, his eyes boring down into her own as he said in a low voice, 'Then here is my answer to your accusation.'

Before she could grasp his meaning he had snatched her to him with a force that not only took her by surprise, but also left her breathless. Her breasts were crushed against him, and as she felt the lines of his lean, hard contours pressing against her own body the blood in her veins exploded into a rushing torrent. Her nerves were shocked and stretched, awakening sensations that until now had been dormant, and she found herself responding to the passion of his kiss. Her arms crept about his neck, while the movement of his lips on her own sent her floating into clouds of bliss.

He released her at last, and for several long moments they stood wrapped in a trance-like silence while an unseen magnet forced them to gaze into each other's eyes. Unspoken words hovered between them until Mary came to her senses with a jolt, and it was then that she felt not only embarrassed, but also infuriated with herself. What in heaven's name had caused her to act in such an uninhibited manner?

'You came to my call,' Justin said, almost as though reading the unspoken question racing about in her mind.

'I—I don't know what you mean,' she prevaricated, turning away from him, yet still aware of the intentness of the dark grey eyes resting upon her face.

'I think you do. I must *call* again some time.' His deep voice remained gentle as it emphasised the word.

'Next time I shall have been warned,' she assured him.

He laughed softly. 'These magic moments are apt to spring upon one as unexpectedly as a thief in the night—and before one can throw up defences. It's the surprise that is inclined to bring forth honesty, as it did moments ago with you.'

She bit her lip while searching for a reply, but could find none.

'I feel sure you were being honest,' he pursued, still watching her closely. 'Or am I wrong about that? Was it, after all, just a cunning act?'

His last words came as a shock, causing her eyes to widen with indignation. 'Cunning act? Towards what purpose?'

'Towards whatever purpose you had in mind for coming here,' he drawled as a soft laugh escaped him.

She felt stunned by the accusation. 'I'm afraid I don't know what you mean. Will you please be more explicit?'

'You must be naïve to imagine I took your reason for being in the orchard for granted. "Just looking— thanks," you said when I found you. For Pete's sake— with so many orchards around Gisborne, why pick on this one?'

Mary felt her cheeks become warm as she sought for a plausible reason, then she said impatiently, 'Can't you understand that I just happened to be passing? When I saw the sign at the gate the name caught my fancy—so I decided to have a closer look.'

His voice hardened. 'Is that the truth, you sly little puss?'

She gasped at the slur in the last words, then decided to ignore it as they gave her the cue for her reply. She would allow him to think that he himself had been the attraction, and, smiling at him, she said, 'Haven't you heard that a cat may look at a *king*?'

He regarded her doubtfully. 'Are you saying you came here to see me? No—I don't believe you,' he declared in a blunt tone. 'There's more to it than that.'

She began to feel apprehensive while wondering to what extent his suspicions were stretching. 'You really think I came here for a special reason?' she queried with a light laugh.

'I do. And if you refuse to bring it out into the open I intend to track it down.'

'How do you propose to do that?' Her voice echoed scorn.

'By having patience—and by giving it time to reveal itself.'

Another laugh escaped her, but this time it was vaguely hysterical. 'Good grief, Mr King—Your Majesty would be better employed in concentrating upon your oranges.'

'That's enough of that particular nonsense,' he snarled, moving towards her again.

'Don't you dare touch me,' she snapped, skipping out of reach, and as she did so she caught sight of her grandfather striding towards them. The evening light and the trees he walked between shadowed his face, but not sufficiently to hide his scowl.

'Brace yourself—trouble is arriving,' Justin remarked calmly.

He was right. Rex Todd's jaw jutted ominously as he approached them. 'Don't you know it's well after six o'clock?' he rasped at Justin. 'You've missed the TV news and Ella's waiting to serve the meal.'

'OK—we're coming,' Justin assured him easily. 'I trust you've had your evening drink,' he added by way of consolation.

'You bet I have. I'm not waiting for people who waste time spooning in the orchard,' he snapped crossly.

Justin grinned. 'Spooning? That word is surely archaic. Mary won't know what it means.'

'I'll warrant she does,' Rex said darkly while favouring Mary with a glittering stare from between narrowed lids.

She returned his gaze unflinchingly. Had he observed their embrace? she wondered. Had he stood concealed by the trees, peering at them through the leaves while watching her response to Justin's kisses? If so, there was nothing she could do about it, although she could understand it had added fuel to his irritation. Naturally, he'd have no desire for her to come between his plans for Justin and Rochelle—and the combining of the orchards.

Justin attempted an explanation. 'I was checking the tangelos.'

Rex snorted. 'Yes, I could see that for myself. They're on the trees, laddie—not on the lassie's lips, in case you're unaware of that fact.'

'So you *were* spying,' Justin snarled.

'Not at all—although I must say I was intrigued by a sight that took me back to my younger days.' He turned and made his way back to the house, leaving them to follow at their leisure.

The action caused Mary to hasten her steps. 'Shouldn't we hurry?' she asked, sending Justin an anxious glance.

His hand on her arm held her back. 'Certainly not. Why should we?'

Her eyes became blue pools that were filled with appeal. 'Please, Justin—are you set on embarrassing me even further?'

He glanced at her briefly as he queried, 'The thought of being caught kissing me has really upset you?'

She spoke coldly. 'In future I'll be grateful if you'll confine your kisses to Rochelle.' It was a lie and she knew it, but for some reason the uttering of the words gave her a perverse satisfaction.

He stopped abruptly, then swung round to face her. 'You really mean that?' he demanded, glaring down into her face.

She nodded, finding herself unable to speak.

His lips twisted while he spoke in a mocking tone. 'Why not be honest and admit it was actually your own response that embarrassed you—plus the fact that it was observed?'

'Can't you understand that such emotions are private?'

'Like your real reason for being here,' he commented drily.

She felt a strong urge to leave him and run towards the house, but to do so would only confirm her guilt. And, after all, her private reason for wishing to be at the Valencia had nothing to do with him. It was the actual property she wished to see—even if the viewing of it included the sight of her grandfather.

When they reached the house Laura greeted them with a smile as she said, 'Ah—there you are. We wondered where you were.'

'Just checking the tangelos,' Justin repeated, sending Rex a hooded glance.

Ella turned to him, her eyes full of innocent surprise. 'I thought you'd already done that with Rochelle. I saw you take her in that direction.'

Justin's mouth tightened. 'That's right, Ella. She had a desire to compare ours with their own fruit. Some orchards ripen more quickly than others—as you know.'

Mary scarcely heard Ella's reply because the latter's information concerning Rochelle had had the effect of leaving her feeling shaken. However, she might have guessed that Justin had already been to the tangelos with his blonde neighbour before guiding herself to that same secluded area, she thought bitterly.

Had he held Rochelle in his arms as closely as he'd held herself? she wondered. Had he kissed Rochelle with as much passion as he'd crushed upon her own lips? The thought sent tremors of anger through her—anger that was sufficiently intense to give her a pain.

And then other questions began to raise their heads— queries such as why she should care about these matters. Was it only her own pride that was at stake—or did the hurt go deeper than mere ego? Granted, she had no wish to think that only a short time previously Justin had kissed Rochelle at the same spot, but what proof did she have that he had actually done so? None at all. It was merely the conclusion she'd jumped to from Ella's remarks.

Vaguely, yet without actually listening, she knew that a discussion had sprung up between Rex, Laura and Ella, and then she became aware that Justin had moved to her side of the living-room. As his arm brushed her sleeve his closeness made her feel weak.

He lowered his head to speak in her ear. 'You're looking very downcast,' he muttered in a low voice. 'May

I ask what depresses you—or is that another private emotion?'

She stopped raking her mind for an answer, then grasped at the one he'd provided. 'Yes—I presume one is permitted to have private thoughts—or does Rochelle tell you everything?' She bit her lip, annoyed with herself for having uttered the blonde's name.

'Ah—the thought of Rochelle irks you somewhat.' He spoke as though he saw the situation clearly.

There and then Mary made a vow that in future she would not allow Ella's remarks to influence her thoughts, and with this decision firmly fixed she resolved to continue work on the memoirs as soon as dinner was finished. The task would remove that devastating man from her sight, and the memory of his kisses from her mind, while the tranquil silence of the study would soothe her ruffled emotions.

And that was another thing—she must stop thinking about that quiet little room as the *study*. It was the *office*—and she'd be wise to remember it—otherwise she might let her mother's old name for it slip off her tongue, and then who knew what suspicions would be stirred in her grandfather's mind?

Later, when she was busy at work, her grandfather came into the room. He said nothing, and from the corner of her eye she saw him gather her typed pages, then settle down to read them. She continued to work, and for the next twenty minutes the silence of the room was broken only by the rustle of paper and the tap-tapping of the typewriter keys.

At last he said, 'You're doing a good job. I'm very pleased with the professional way you've set it out.' Then, after a brief hesitation, he asked, 'Do you find it to be fairly—readable?'

'Yes. It flows—and I find it interesting, but——'

He eyed her sharply. 'But what? Don't be afraid to speak up.'

'But I also find it rather lacking.'

The beatled grey brows drew together. '*Lacking*? What the devil do you mean by lacking?'

She felt like one who had slapped another person's child, but she battled on bravely. 'It's impersonal. There are no human touches in it, and that makes it seem cold.'

'Cold to whom? Who wants human touches in it?'

'Any publisher who happens to see it. It's a mass of bald facts, and although they are your memoirs you don't seem to feature among them at all. They're the strangest memoirs I've ever seen,' she informed him bluntly.

His scowl deepened. 'You're an expert on what publishers want?'

'I'm not entirely ignorant about the subject.' She went on to explain her job with the literary agent, then returned to the text before her. 'This reads more like a history of citrus-growing in the Gisborne district than a man's recollections. For instance, I've not yet come across a single reference to family. Have you never had children of your own?' She held her breath while waiting for his answer.

'I have no family,' he almost snarled. 'Only Laura and Justin.'

'Really?' she said, finding difficulty in keeping sarcasm from her tone, then warned herself to keep her temper, otherwise she'd reveal more than she intended. Then she nodded towards the portrait. 'Doesn't she warrant a mention in your memoirs?'

He raised his eyes to meet the blue ones above the mantelpiece. 'She's in my heart. I don't need her on paper.'

Mary thought, Then you do have a heart? But aloud she said, 'I'm glad you're satisfied with what I've done so far——'

'Which is quite enough for today.' The voice that spoke from the doorway belonged to Justin, who turned a stern glance upon Rex. 'Don't you think she's done enough for today—or are you still cracking the whip over her head?'

Mary felt a protest was necessary. 'He's *not* cracking the whip. He hasn't even started to do so——'

Justin grinned. 'Give him time and you'll find yourself doing exactly as he wishes. You'll be toeing the line with the rest of us.'

Rex cocked an eyebrow at Mary. 'Something tells me that Justin has other plans for you, like a moonlight walk in the orchard—towards the tangelos,' he added slyly.

CHAPTER FIVE

MARY'S heart skipped a beat while she felt herself go hot. So her grandfather *had* seen Justin kissing her, she realised, and she could only stare at him wordlessly.

Justin also appeared to realise that they had been observed, but in no way did it seem to concern him. 'You do have good ideas, Rex, but actually it's not what I had in mind.'

'No? So what did you have in mind?' the old man queried. 'I'm sure Mary will be interested.'

'Work.' Justin snapped the word abruptly.

'Oh—you mean office work? You intend to remain in here with her?' His lips tightened beneath the grey moustache.

'That's right,' Justin informed him easily. 'There's the small matter of the accounts—those things that must be paid each month. You might recall that it's my night for attending to them.' He turned to Mary. 'You'll not object if I see to the clerical side of the orchard?'

'Of course not,' she muttered faintly, not knowing whether she felt relieved or disappointed at not being led towards the trees.

'I promise not to disturb you,' Justin said.

'See that you keep that promise,' Rex growled as he sent a penetrating glance from Justin to Mary before leaving the room.

But Justin did disturb her, far more than she cared to admit even to herself. She knew he was sitting at the desk with his back turned towards her, and although her own back was turned to him she was vitally conscious of his presence.

80

True to his promise, he made no attempt to converse with her—a fact which frustrated her because he seemed able to ignore her so easily. To him—obviously—she wasn't even in the room. Well, it was a game that two could play. He shall speak *first*, she told herself with angry determination, then channelled her mind into the effort of deciphering the pages lying beside her.

But the room did not remain entirely silent because the typewriter chattered as she touched the keys, and from the desk came the whisper of rustling papers. Was he as engrossed as he appeared? she wondered. Or was he waiting for her own work to stop?

The answer came a short time later when she had taken up a pen to reconstruct a sentence without altering its meaning. She noticed that the rustling of the papers had ceased, and then the silence was broken by the movement of the desk chair. The sound made her feel tense, and she wondered if he intended to leave the room without a word. Nor did she allow herself to look round to ascertain his intentions.

Instead she forced the pen to glide across the scribbling-pad, but found that the right words evaded her mind. She sat, tense, while listening for his exit from the room, and then a gasp escaped her as she felt his hands creep round her waist to cup her breasts. His thumbs stroked her nipples, which immediately hardened into tight rosebuds and sent quivers shooting through her body.

Startled, she dropped the pen and gripped his wrists in an effort to remove his hands, but his superior strength proved to be too much for her. 'Stop it!' she hissed furiously. 'Don't you dare touch me in this manner.'

His lips caressed her ear. 'You were ready to be touched this afternoon,' he murmured, unperturbed. 'And look at you now—nipples as firm as crimson berries about to be nibbled——'

'You know nothing about my—my—about any part of me,' she lashed at him.

He chuckled, then spoke huskily. 'Sooner or later there'll be a much closer encounter, and I think you know it.'

A flush rose to her cheeks as she wrenched herself free of his hands by springing to her feet. 'I know nothing of the sort. You're jumping to conclusions,' she declared, twisting round to face him.

He ignored her denial, his expression changing as a thought appeared to strike him. 'Encounter—is that it?' he mused. 'Is it possible you hoped to meet somebody in the orchard?'

She gaped at him. 'What put such an idea into your head?'

'Well—you did say a cat could look at a king. Is it possible that this particular kitten *was* searching for my humble self?'

She stared at him, wide-eyed. 'Are you accusing me of coming to find *you*? My oath, you flatter yourself,' she flared in a fury.

'There's no need to get so uptight about it,' he assured her in a mild tone. 'It wouldn't be the first time a lady had glanced in my direction—even if I say it myself,' he added modestly.

Mary could believe it, but had no intention of voicing the fact; therefore she merely looked at him in silence.

He went on, his face serious, his eyes almost boring into her own. 'What's the matter with you? You weren't like this in the orchard. Why this sudden stand-offishness?'

She became tense as she remembered his arms holding her against him. 'The orchard was a mistake,' she said in a low voice. 'I hope you realise we were observed.'

'So what? It might help him to get off my back where Rochelle is concerned.' His tone had become nonchalant.

'Then it is true? He is bent on seeing you married to her?'

'I'll admit he's trying to be subtle over the job, but he's about as subtle as an elephant in the flower garden.'

Mary felt frustrated as she snapped, 'Well, that—that orchard episode must not happen again.'

'Of course it'll happen again. I intend to kiss you again—and again—have no doubt about *that*.'

She became impatient. 'Can't you understand that we could be observed again? Or are you intent upon embarrassing me?'

'Why should it embarrass you?' he demanded coolly.

'Because it makes me look cheap, of course,' she flung at him.

'I can't see that a kiss should have such a devastating effect.'

'Can't you? Then hear this.' A deep breath betrayed her indignation. 'The observer—whoever he or she happens to be—will know that the kiss will be completely without real depth or feeling.'

He regarded her with interest. 'Is that so? You're saying the observer will be clairvoyant?'

'Of course not,' she retorted scornfully. 'I mean the person who is likely to see us will know you well enough to have heard of your intentions to remain fancy-free. If you've already told me of that fact, you'll have mentioned it to others,' she added pointedly.

His tone became cool. 'Go on—something tells me there's more.'

'There certainly is,' she flung at him, her anger rising. 'The observer will also guess that for your part the kiss is merely a preliminary to the—the more intimate plans you have in mind. I shall be looked upon as a poor, dumb, silly twit who has fallen beneath the spell of the orchard king, and quite incapable of resisting your advances. In short—he or she will have us in bed together——' She stopped with a gasp, shocked by the lack of control of her own babbling tongue.

'What an excellent idea!' he exclaimed. Then his face became serious as his voice softened. 'Shall we go now?'

She felt dazed. 'What? Go where?'

'To bed, of course.'

'Certainly not—and don't you dare make such a suggestion!' The words came with a gasp of fury as her cheeks turned crimson.

'Oh, well—later, perhaps. In the meantime shall we continue with the—er—preliminary treatment?' And before she could move away his arms had reached out to draw her closer to him.

Bereft of words and overcome by a sudden fatigue brought on by the build-up of her own emotions, she leaned against him unresistingly, her forehead nestling against his neck. His fingers beneath her chin tilted her face upwards, and she could only stare mutely into the dark grey eyes gazing down into her own.

He said, 'If you really don't want me to kiss you I shall not do so. Nor shall I ever make another attempt to do so.'

She stared back at him wordlessly. How stupid— how *stupid* could she be? She *longed* for him to kiss her——

Taking her silence for assent, he lowered his head until his lips rested upon the softness of her mouth. She did not have the strength to deny the closeness of his embrace, and as she closed her eyes she felt the blood rush in her veins.

It was a gentle kiss without the pressure of passion, and, while she waited for it to deepen, this did not happen. Instead she found herself subjected to a tender nuzzling which left her in a frustrated state of longing to feel his arms tighten about her body. And, although they did not, Justin seemed to be in no hurry to end the kiss.

And then the sound of a cough coming from the direction of the passage caused her to leap away from him. She swung around, expecting to see her grandfather in the doorway, but the space was empty. 'Who was that?' she gasped in a breathless tone.

'Old Rex. He just passed,' Justin informed her nonchalantly.

'He—*he saw us!*' she exclaimed, aghast at the thought.

'I suppose so.' The words were accompanied by a slight lift of his shoulders as he eyed her with amusement.

'You *knew* he was there,' she accused furiously.

'I suspected he might be—hovering,' he admitted shamelessly.

'Which means that you deliberately set out to—to embarrass me—*again*. It was a—a premeditated act to make me feel mortified. Well, you've certainly succeeded.' She almost choked on the words.

'You're entirely wrong,' he gritted. 'I merely decided to drop a hint that I like having you around.'

'Why bother to lie to him? You know you don't like having me around. You're suspicious of me. You're sure I have an ulterior motive for being here—and now you're hoping Mr Todd will see a good reason for giving me my marching orders.'

'Got it all worked out, have you?'

'It hasn't been difficult to do so. He won't realise you're merely *using* me to thwart his plans where Rochelle is concerned,' she pointed out. 'But until he tells me to go I'll stay with the job until it's finished. After that I'll be off. Smartly.'

'I trust not before you've told me what you were searching for in the orchard,' he said silkily.

Mary glared at him without speaking, then left the room. Had she found more than she'd bargained for in the orchard? Granted, it had satisfied her curiosity concerning her mother's old home. And it had at least given her a partial glimpse of her roots in the form of her grandfather. But had it also brought her in contact with a man she'd be unable to forget?

The next week passed without incident mainly because Mary scarcely left the office, and Justin failed to go near it. And while his persistent absence frustrated her, she made a valiant effort to put him out of her mind. Of course she saw him at mealtimes, when he directed most of his conversation towards Rex, but the moment dinner was over she returned to the office, nursing a feeling of having been deliberately ignored.

On one occasion he came to the office door and stood watching her for several moments. She turned and looked at him, waiting for him to speak, but he remained silent then disappeared. Had he been waiting for *her* to speak first? she wondered. Her eyes filled with tears that were brushed away angrily while she told herself not to be idiotic.

And then came the day when Ella discovered the pantry shelves were so lacking in marmalade that there was barely enough for the next morning's breakfast. She appeared at the office door with a basket in her hand and a look of appeal on her face.

'I'm in a fix, dear,' she said to Mary. 'I wondered if you'd help me? It won't take long.'

Mary stood up, thankful to be given a reason to do something different for a change. 'Of course I'll help you. What would you like me to do?' she asked willingly.

'I need fruit for marmalade, but I have cookies in the oven and more waiting to go in. Laura would fetch it for me if she were here, but she's visiting Rochelle's mother. I wondered if you'd——'

'Fetch the fruit? Of course—no trouble at all. What do you need and where shall I find it?'

'You'll have to go out into the orchard and find Justin. Just ask him for marmalade fruit and he'll give you four grapefruit that are still partly green, two Lisbon lemons and an orange.'

Mary stared at Ella without moving. 'Go and find Justin,' she'd said. It was the last thing she wished to do, she told herself—or was it the thing she wished to do most? After all, it might cause that wall to come tumbling down—that invisible barrier that seemed to have risen between them. She took the basket and made her way towards the orchard.

As she walked out into the green world of the trees she listened for the sound of voices which would lead her in the right direction, but as she moved from one row to another even the twittering of the birds seemed to have been silenced.

For a short time she stood nonplussed until suddenly the sound of the tractor came to her ears from only a couple of rows away. Relieved, she moved towards it, only to find her grandfather in charge of the group of pickers. No wonder the place was silent, she thought.

Rex remained motionless while watching her approach, then he moved the tractor and fruit-laden trailer further along the row before coming to speak to her. 'You were looking for me?' he asked gruffly, his blue eyes raking her appearance as she stood before him.

She almost quailed before the intentness of his searching gaze. 'No—I'm looking for Justin. He knows the right fruit for Ella's marmalade. She's almost out of it.'

'That's no good. Breakfast isn't breakfast without marmalade. Well, I suppose you needed to stretch your legs,' he admitted grudgingly. 'You'll find him over by the boundary fence. He's talking to his—friend.'

'You mean, Rochelle?'

'That's right. She came to say she had news for him.'

'I won't interrupt his conversation for long—but Ella needs the fruit.'

'I'm sure she does,' the old man retorted. 'She knows my mood when I have to use honey or Marmite instead of marmalade on my toast.'

She sent him one of her sweetest smiles. 'Many would be thankful just to have the toast.' Then she left him and went towards the boundary fence, where she found Rochelle and Justin, the former standing on her parents' side of the dividing line of wires and battens. Even from the distance she could see the contrast in their expressions—Justin's somewhat grim while Rochelle's held a hint of satisfaction.

However, this switched to a sullen look as she drew near, but Justin's expression did not change. And when she handed him the basket with Ella's request he continued to regard her in glum silence. It was almost sufficiently antagonistic to make her suspect their conversation had concerned herself.

'Marmalade grapefruit,' Rochelle sneered as Justin strode away with the basket. 'That was merely an excuse to come searching for Justin. Ella is *never* out of marmalade. It'd be more than her life is worth——'

'I don't have to listen to your comments,' Mary snapped, then turned and ran after Justin.

But Rochelle was over the fence in a flash, and, racing after Mary, she caught up with her and grabbed her arm. 'You came here to spy on us,' she panted in a fury.

'Don't be stupid,' Mary gasped, wrenching her arm free from the other's hold.

'What the hell's going on?' The roar came from Rex, who pushed his way through the trees, causing the ripe fruit to drop.

Rochelle swung round to face him. 'She's spying on Justin and me,' she complained in an aggrieved voice.

Rex looked at her reflectively. 'I doubt it,' he said at last. 'Mary didn't know where to find Justin until I told her. Why don't you run away home? I'm sure there are things you could be doing for your mother.'

Rochelle changed her tune while smiling winningly at the old man. 'Yes, of course—I'm always busy doing things for Mother. Please tell Justin I'll be home this evening and that I'll expect to see him later.' Then, with her head held high, she left them.

Mary looked at Rex gratefully. 'Thank you for saving me. I'm sure she was about to claw my eyes out.'

His voice softened. 'I wouldn't like to see anything happen to those particular eyes. They're so similar to my own dear Mary's.'

His tone and words amazed her, making her feel that perhaps he was human after all. But possibly the greatest shock was the fact that he'd actually supported her against Rochelle—*Rochelle* whom he wished to see established in the homestead as Justin's wife.

And then Justin joined them, the basket on his arm filled with the required varieties of fruit. 'There's enough here for a couple of boilings of marmalade,' he told Mary, his face still unsmiling.

'Thank you. Ella will be pleased,' she said, reaching to take the basket.

He waved her hand aside. 'It's heavy. I'll carry it back to the house for you.'

'Thank you,' she said again, and after that they walked in a silence that was almost depressing. Something is bugging him, she thought. Something that Rochelle has said—and of course it concerns *me*. Should she demand an explanation? No—let him think or believe as he wished.

When they reached the kitchen Ella had the last tray of cookies cooling on a rack. Justin placed the basket on the table and said with what sounded like forced cheerfulness, 'There you are, Ella. I hope they're just as you like them—not too ripe.' He then helped himself to a peanut brownie.

The small woman spoke quickly. 'I was so glad to be able to send Mary, especially as I had all these cookies on hand.' She paused to send him a significant look. 'And you know what Rex is like when there's no marmalade for breakfast.'

'Only too well, but we won't go into details,' Justin grinned. He turned to Mary. 'And now I presume you'll rush back to your typewriter——'

'While you'll rush back to your friend,' she cut in. 'Was her news exciting?' she asked, hoping he would drop a hint concerning it, or even just a word to indicate that it did not involve herself.

'How do you know she had news?' he demanded sharply.

'Mr Todd told me when I was searching for you. And in case he forgets to tell you, she expects you to call upon her this evening.'

'Does she, indeed?'

'Of course you'll be there—at the double.' Mary was unable to keep the sardonic note from her voice.

'You appear to have my relationship with Rochelle completely cut and dried,' he lashed at her in sudden anger.

She was surprised by his wrath but managed a casual shrug as she said, 'It appears to be what everyone expects——'

'Everyone except myself,' he snarled, then strode from the room.

At that moment Ella came to the bench and began to slice the washed fruit. Mary lifted a knife to help her, and as she did so the strangest feeling came over her. It was almost as if she'd been there before, although she knew that this was impossible. However, she also knew that she was standing where her mother had stood, no doubt attending to this same task—and years earlier her grandmother would also have sliced the fruit for marmalade.

Sadly she thought, I'm the third generation to stand at this bench—and Grandfather doesn't know it. Would he ever learn of it? Would it mean anything to him? She doubted it. And then Justin's voice jolted her out of the daydream.

He had entered the kitchen unheard and now stood beside her. 'I thought I'd come back,' he said, despite Ella's presence.

'Oh? Why?' She looked at him blankly, awaiting further explanation while becoming conscious of her own quickened breath.

Ella said hastily, 'I'll go to the pantry and weigh the sugar. And I'd better put the cookies out of Justin's reach.'

As Ella disappeared Justin went on, 'I fear I was somewhat abrupt with you.'

'You've been abrupt with me for most of the week. I've become accustomed to it.' Her eyes were wide with reproach.

He lowered his voice, his handsome face holding an expression of concern. 'This afternoon your spirits appeared to be at a lower ebb than usual. Care to tell me why?'

Mary thought for several moments before she said in a voice that was slightly unsteady, 'I don't usually jump over the moon when poisonous tongues are at work on my behalf. Nor does it amuse me to be accused of spying on you and—and your girlfriend.' She paused, then felt she had to know. 'Did *you* think I was spying?'

'Of course not. The idea is ridiculous.'

'That's all right, then. What *she* thinks doesn't matter.'

He placed a hand on her shoulder, his touch almost giving her an electric shock. 'Are you saying that what I think *does* matter?'

'I'm not allowing it to matter,' she managed to say loftily, although she wasn't too sure of this fact. 'But I would like to know—just from sheer curiosity—why you have been so abrupt all this week.'

'Because you're one big question mark hanging over my head,' he told her frankly. 'You niggle at me.'

'Thank you. You do say the nicest things. Is this your way of lifting my spirits?'

He ignored the taunt. 'There's definitely a reason for your presence here—and if only you'd come out into the open and tell me what it is——'

'You'd go laughing and dancing from tree to tree. Is that it?'

'I'll admit I'd feel happier.'

'And less worried about my integrity?' A deep hurt filled her as she asked, 'Why can't you trust me? Why can't you believe that I just wanted to walk in the orchard?'

'Because I can't help feeling there's more to it than that.'

For one brief moment she contemplated confiding in him, but fear of his reaction kept her silent. It would prove his suspicions to be correct, and she could almost guess at the thoughts that would revolve in his mind.

A walk in the orchard? I *knew* there was more to it than that, he would claim with a sense of triumph. You are here to ingratiate yourself with your grandfather. No doubt you've been sent by your mother, who is planning to share in his estate. It's possible the idea has been put into her head by the death of your father's mother. Oh, yes—I can see it all, he would say.

And, thinking about it, Mary realised that to Justin the picture would be all too clear.

His voice cut into her thoughts. 'What's going on in your head?'

'Only bitterness,' she admitted, suddenly aware of the truth of this fact.

'Then spit it out,' he advised. 'Rid yourself of it—or at least share it.'

She shook her head and was then relieved of further discussion by Ella's return from the pantry.

The small woman placed a large bowl of sugar on the table, then turned anxious eyes towards Mary as she said, 'Rex is on his way back to the house. I saw him through the pantry window. If he finds you in the kitchen doing my work I'll be in deep trouble.'

'OK—I'll go back to the office,' Mary said. She gave her hands a hurried rinse and a quick dab with a towel, then fled from the room as Rex stepped on to the back veranda.

Justin followed her at a leisurely pace, reaching her side as she rolled a clean sheet of white paper into the typewriter. 'Do I detect fear on your part where Rex is concerned?' he drawled.

'Certainly not. It's just that I don't want his wrath to descend upon Ella,' she explained apprehensively.

'Ella is not employed by Rex. She's employed by me as a companion-help to my aunt.'

Mary felt puzzled. 'But Ella said she'd be in deep trouble.'

'Only because she was keeping you from the typewriter. He's dead keen to see this job finished.'

'That makes two of us,' she flashed at him. 'I'm more than anxious to finish it—and then I can be on my way and out of sight of those who imagine I'm here with an ulterior motive.' The last words were uttered with a slight tilt of the chin.

Justin stepped closer and looked down into her face. 'I seem to have stepped off on the wrong foot where you're concerned.'

She was unable to conceal her surprise. 'Good grief—do I detect the admission of a mistake coming from a man?'

His lips twitched. 'Strangely enough, men do make mistakes.'

'But they never admit it—even unto the end,' she remarked in a solemn voice.

'You're thinking of one man in particular?'

She turned away from him. 'Yes—you could say so.'

'Care to tell me about it? I'm a good listener.'

'In this case, I would doubt it. Now—if you'll excuse me—I'd like to get on with this job. I'd be most upset if my parents decided they're ready to go home before it's finished.'

'Well, when you feel like talking about this particular man, just say the word.' Unexpectedly his hands went to her shoulders while he bent his head and swiftly brushed her lips with his own. Then he almost pushed her away from him and left the room.

The action made her nerves tingle, and she found herself wishing the caress had been less brief. She also found herself gripped by a sudden yearning to be held close to him, and only with an effort did she shake herself out of a daze and sit at the typewriter, where she dragged her thoughts back to their former conversation about a particular man who, of course, was her grandfather.

Staring at the half-typed page before her, she gave a long sigh as she realised the futility of talking about the situation with Justin. He would believe only the old man's side of the story.

And now that she had met her grandfather he was no longer a nebulous ogre. Nevertheless she could well imagine how he'd ranted and raved over her mother's marriage to Alan Healey. She could almost hear his roar when he'd told her mother to get down the road—just as he would to any member of the staff—and never show her face again. And Mother had gone. And had not shown her face again.

Then, as the years had passed and she'd failed to return to see him—as perhaps he'd secretly expected—he'd considered himself to have been deserted. And that was what he'd told Justin.

Mary gave another sigh, saddened by the thought that after such a long time her mother and grandfather were now only a few miles from each other, yet still so far away in their relationship. But what could she do about it?

Would it be possible to contrive an opportunity to bring them together, even if only briefly? Would the barrier between them be broken—or would Rex Todd reject his daughter again? Mary had no wish to see her mother put through such an ordeal; therefore she began to listen to the part of her brain which whispered about letting sleeping dogs lie.

And then she came to a decision. When she'd finished the job she'd admit her identity to her grandfather, and his reaction would no doubt give her the cue for any further move. But until then she'd be wise to stop wasting time by daydreaming in this manner. At least she'd been given the opportunity to see the Valencia, and for that she'd always be grateful.

For the next few days Mary made every effort to eliminate the thoughts of other people from her mind, but where Justin was concerned her attempts were a miserable failure. His face continued to hover above the typewriter, and she found herself constantly listening for his approach. Then, when he did come, she felt cross because he had taken so long about it.

'This is a surprise,' she said with forced sweetness when she looked up to discover him standing in the doorway.

He sent her a long searching glance then admitted, 'I've felt worried about you. At mealtimes your eyes have looked tired, and I know you've had your nose to the grindstone non-stop. Rex is more than delighted with you—in case he hasn't bothered to tell you.'

She felt pleased. 'He is? Actually, he's said very little.'

'It'd kill him to give praise.'

'He comes in each evening to read over what I've typed during the day, but so far there have been no complaints.'

'I've just told that old slave-driver that I intend forcing you to stretch your legs in the afternoon sunshine.'

'Really? How do you propose to do that?' She turned in her seat to regard him with interest, at the same time feeling secretly pleased to find him concerned on her behalf.

'By taking you for a walk in the fresh air. I doubt that you've even seen inside the packing shed.'

'I peeped in one day,' she admitted. 'But they all looked to be so busy that I didn't dare intrude to ask how everything worked.'

'Then it's time you had a guided tour. The packing shed is an important part of the citrus orchard you were so anxious to examine,' he said with a tinge of amusement in his voice.

'I know you're laughing at me,' she flashed at him while resentment bubbled. 'And it may also amuse you to learn that I've now realised my interest in citrus orchards was a mistake.'

'Oh? Why would that be?' he drawled.

'Because it has caused me unnecessary mental distress,' she admitted frankly. 'Your suspicions and your distrust of me have been too apparent for words.'

'Come now, aren't you exaggerating——?'

'Definitely not. That first day—when you found me in the orchard—I had intended taking only a quick peep and then to go on my way. But you offered to show me more, and I couldn't resist. And then the question of Rex's memoirs arose——'

'And again you couldn't resist because they gave you the chance to wriggle into the household.' His words held a sardonic ring.

She seethed with anger. '*Wriggle*? How *dare* you make such an accusation? However, it does prove that your attitude towards me has been thoroughly *rotten*. From the moment I offered to type the memoirs there's been an undercurrent of antagonism between us. Your suspicions that I have an ulterior motive for being here stick out a mile. Your distrust of me is positively *sickening*,' she hissed, then found herself having to pause for breath.

His mouth tightened. 'Well, now, with that lot off your chest I'm sure you feel much better. Shall we go to the packing shed?'

They walked along the path in silence, and as they reached the large timber-built shed he paused to demand, 'Have you simmered down—or do you intend shouting your grievances to the staff?'

'Of course I won't,' she retorted scornfully. 'But if you're worried about it there's no need for you to waste your precious time in showing me——'

'I believe I can spare a few minutes,' he cut in, then added drily, 'I'll even show you the fertiliser shed as a bonus for good behaviour.' He then ushered her into the shed.

Mary's irritations dropped away from her as she gazed at the scene so accurately described by her mother. A swift glance took in the roller conveyor which carried the fruit through the cleaning and waxing process, and from it her eyes went to the grading belt upon which the golden balls passed before a line of women whose gloved hands reached to cull them into separate grades. The speed with which the packers wrapped each fruit in a square of white paper amazed her, and as they left the shed she turned to Justin gratefully. 'Thank you for showing it to me—it was really most interesting.'

'I trust you'll find the fertiliser shed to be equally intriguing,' he said gravely, although his lips twitched as he led her towards a small building which nestled beneath ancient macrocarpa trees a distance beyond the garages.

It took several minutes to reach it, and as they drew near she exclaimed, 'I hadn't noticed this shed previously, but then it's quite a distance from the house.'

'It's fairly isolated,' he admitted. 'But that's how I like it, because its seclusion enables me to experiment without interruption.'

'Ah—then you *do* have a secret formula for fertilising the oranges. Rochelle mentioned it—remember?'

'By pure luck I believe I have hit on a good mixture, but I've no intention of making it public.' He ushered her into the shed, where large sacks, bulging with different types of fertilisers, leaned drunkenly against the walls or were stacked upon each other. There was a weighing machine and a contrivance for mixing the contents of the sacks, while on the bench were books containing records of the amounts used in various parts of the orchard.

Mary noticed a sack standing apart from the rest. She bent to read its label then said, 'Valencia Mix? Is this your own special brew for the orange trees?'

He nodded. 'That's it. Somewhat smelly, I'm afraid.'

'It must be fun to watch things develop each year—especially the blossoms appearing and later turning into green marbles. Do you feel the orchard is a living thing—and that the trees are like people who stand waiting to be fed, otherwise they're unable to produce?'

He looked at her intently, then admitted, 'I'm surprised that you should say that. It's a feeling I've had for a long time.'

A smile lit her face as a thought struck her. 'It's said that the Saracen brides wore orange blossom to indicate the hope of fruitfulness. Apparently in their part of the world no tree was more prolific in its bearing.' Her smile broadened as she added, 'It's also said that if a man gathers orange blossom it means he's looking for a wife. Is this why you're taking such care of the orange trees near the boundary?'

'Who says I'm taking special care of those particular trees?' Justin demanded testily. 'I haven't divulged what I'm doing.'

'It was just that Rochelle mentioned that they seemed to be larger than their own. Hadn't her mother noticed the difference between the size of your oranges and the ones on their side of the fence?'

'I suppose it's possible. Actually I used those trees in my experiments because they're on the end of the rows, which made it more convenient to watch their progress.'

'And also more convenient to hand a branch of lovely orange blossom across the fence,' Mary remarked, then immediately felt furious with herself.

His brows rose as he regarded her with interest. 'The thought of it would concern you—or perhaps even upset you?'

'Of course not,' she retorted scornfully. 'How could it possibly concern, much less *upset* me? You've got to be joking!'

'Yet the thought did spring into your head,' he persisted.

'I'm sorry—it was just a stupid, facetious remark that I had no right to make,' she said, still annoyed with herself.

He moved closer to take her face between his two hands, then his eyes became serious as they gazed intently into her own. His voice remained low as he said,

'If I present a branch laden with orange blossom to you, would it all blow back in my face?'

Her breath had quickened at the feel of his touch on her cheeks. Her heart had begun to thump while waiting for the kiss she felt sure was only moments away, yet she controlled her quivering senses as she said, 'I'll be home in Sydney before the trees are in full bloom.'

He frowned. 'You sound as if you're keen to get there.'

'I'm hoping I can finish the memoirs before my parents decide they're ready to leave for Australia.'

His mouth twisted slightly. 'You're hinting you'd like to rush back to the typewriter. OK—I'll let you get on with the job.'

His hands dropped to his sides, leaving her with a feeling of anticlimax.

CHAPTER SIX

MARY turned away, fearful that her eyes would betray her disappointment. She took a deep breath, and in an effort to appear normal she said, 'Thank you for showing me the packing shed activities—and for confiding that you really have been experimenting. That's the second time.'

Justin's brows rose. 'The second time for what?'

'For private disclosure. The first time was when you told me why you're so determined to remain fancy-free—but never fear, I shall respect both confidences.'

'Thank you. I'm not in the habit of airing my secrets. In fact I'm puzzled to know how you dragged it out of me.'

She laughed. 'I did nothing of the kind. You told me of your own free will. And as for your experiments, you led me in here. I didn't even know the shed existed.'

'I suppose you're right,' he muttered.

She spoke earnestly. 'Remember, if ever you visit Sydney, please get in touch and tell me how successful the Valencia Mix is proving to be.'

'You're suggesting you'd be interested?'

'*Of course* I'd be interested. After staying here how could I be uninterested?' She paused, then tried to keep the ring of hope from her voice as she asked, 'Do you ever make a trip across the Tasman?'

'My last trip was three years ago when old Rex persuaded me to go to Queensland.'

'Ah—a fact-finding mission on the growing of mandarins?'

'You could say it was fact-finding, but it had nothing to do with fruit. It was to do with——' He fell silent.

100

Mary felt herself go tense, instinct warning that if she showed too much curiosity he would remain silent; therefore she said, 'I hope the mission was successful.'

'It wasn't,' he snapped, irritated by the memory. 'It was a confounded waste of time on my part just when the busy season was about to begin.'

She said nothing, but waited hopefully.

He went on impatiently, the memory evidently goading him to further revelation, 'OK—as I've already given you two confidences I might as well present you with the third. It happened after Rochelle's parents, Susan and Bob Grover, had taken a trip to Brisbane and the Gold Coast. On their return Susan came rushing to Rex in a frenzy of excitement. She had seen Elizabeth, the daughter who had deserted him—or so she claimed.'

Mary kept her mouth shut, but only with an effort.

Justin went on, 'Apparently it was during a rush-hour in the centre of Brisbane, and by the time Susan had pushed her way through the crowd Elizabeth had disappeared.'

'I see. So what happened?' Mary queried, recalling the holiday they'd had on the Gold Coast three years ago.

'Unfortunately Susan lost her completely, but on her return she couldn't get to Rex quickly enough to report that Elizabeth was now living in Brisbane.'

Mary smiled inwardly, realising the mistake that had been made. 'How did Mr Todd react?' she asked. 'Didn't you say her name was not to be mentioned?'

'That's right. Well—he went through a short period of being very quiet until one day he approached me with the request to go to Brisbane to see if I could contact her.'

'He did?' Mary tried to disguise the pleasure she felt. So her grandfather had actually held out a hand—even if it had been Justin's hand. 'But you were unable to find her?'

'Yes—I made every effort in Brisbane but was unable to trace Elizabeth Healey.'

And no wonder, Mary thought. She hasn't been Elizabeth Healey for *years*. Aloud she said, 'So you came home admitting defeat.'

'Yes.' He paused then said ruefully, 'I'm afraid Rex was disappointed. He became depressed and was thoroughly annoyed with himself for having persuaded me to make the effort to find her. His attitude reverted to his former one of refusing to hear her name mentioned.'

'You're saying that what was dead came to life briefly—then died again?'

'That's about it. If he learns I've told you he'll murder me.'

'He'll not learn of it from me,' she promised.

'Good. I know I can rely on you.'

'That's a change from wondering about my ulterior motive for being here,' she said pointedly.

'I'll admit I'm moving away from that trend of thought.'

'Poor Mr King—your mind must be quite muddled about me.'

'Yes, you can say *that* again—it damn well is.'

'Then I'll get back to the job so that I can complete it and disappear from your sight for all time.' She moved towards the door of the fertiliser shed, then paused to look back and add, 'I'm sure you'll be more than relieved.'

He made no comment, nor did he move to detain her.

As she walked back towards the house Mary became conscious of a descending gloom, and although she listened hopefully for the sound of following footsteps on the gravel near the garages there was nothing to be heard. OK, so he was letting her go to get on with the job because this was the only way to hasten her departure.

But if this was his wish why did he cause interruptions by taking her to see the packing and fertiliser sheds? And what had prompted him to confide in her? He was a complex man, she sensed—yet she felt irresistibly drawn towards him; therefore the sooner she left the Valencia the less vulnerable she'd be to his undeniable charms. And with this decision made she almost rushed into the office.

During the next few days Mary's fingers scarcely left the keys of the little portable machine, and suddenly she began to see that the end of the job was in sight. The pile of papers on the desk was now rapidly diminishing to a small stack, and she wasn't sure whether to be relieved or sorry.

On one occasion Justin came into the office, his face unsmiling as he put a question to her. 'Would you care to come for a walk in the orchard? You've been going non-stop.'

She longed to go with him but she remained firm. Shaking her head, she said, 'Thank you for the thought—but if you'll excuse me I'd prefer to continue with this.'

His mouth tightened. 'You mean you've no wish to come with me?'

'I didn't say that. I mean I'm near enough to the finish to be seeing light at the end of the tunnel.'

'Very well. Please yourself,' he snapped curtly, then left the office with barely concealed irritation.

After his departure she wondered why she had refused to go with him, then honesty forced her to admit that Justin was having an effect upon her. When he drew near her heart thumped, while even the sound of his voice made her feel slightly breathless. Memory of his kisses sent tingles through her entire being, causing her to suspect she was on the verge of falling in love with this man who, by his own admission, was determined to remain fancy-free.

But, being a red-blooded man, he was not immune to kissing a girl, and to feeling the softness of a body close to his own. Hadn't he warned that the time would come when he'd fondle her breasts and nibble her nipples? Berries, he'd called them. And this could happen in a secluded part of the orchard where ripe oranges hung in the boughs above—until one dropped on his head. The thought broke the daydream. It made her laugh and brought her back to her senses.

But, while Justin made no further attempt to disturb her work, it had an interruption she was unable to refuse. It occurred one afternoon when Laura came to the office door.

Smiling, the older woman said, 'My dear, I have a visitor who would like to meet you. Ella has just taken tea into the living-room. I'd be so pleased if you'd join us.'

The words were spoken calmly enough, but they sounded more like a command than an invitation, and for some vague reason they filled Mary with apprehension. During her period at the Valencia she had been aware of various visitors in the living-room, but this was the first time she had been requested to meet any of them. However, she had no option but to do so, and after all a short break with social chat would be a pleasant change.

When she entered the living-room a woman with light-coloured hair and pale grey eyes stared at her with unconcealed interest. Mary thought she looked vaguely familiar, and then the reason for this became clear when Laura made the introduction which immediately put Mary on her guard.

'Susan, this is Mary Kendall, who is typing Rex's memoirs—and this is Rochelle's mother, Mrs Grover——'

The pale grey eyes continued to dissect every detail of Mary's appearance, then the lips thinned as Susan Grover said in a cool tone, 'Really! I *must* say Rochelle was most disappointed when Rex saw fit to hand his memoirs to a stranger—although I *must* say you don't look like a stranger. You're *so* like someone I used to know.'

Mary smiled as she took the tea Laura had poured. 'Isn't there an old story about everyone having a double somewhere in the world?'

'An old wives' tale,' Susan retorted. 'Hereditary bone-structure is what makes people look alike——' She broke off as Justin came into the room, then cooed, 'Ah, Justin, dear—how nice to see you at last. You haven't been near us for *ages*.'

'Rochelle didn't come with you,' he observed casually.

'No. The *dear* child is *so* busy working in the orchard. She's *always* working in the orchard—but of course it will belong to her some day,' Susan added on a careless note.

'That day is surely a long way off,' Laura put in.

'Not as far as you would imagine,' Susan said in a confidential tone. 'Bob is thinking of retiring across the Tasman—on the *Gold Coast*, you know—and then he'll hand it all over to Rochelle.'

'How nice for her,' Justin remarked.

'Bob's confident that you'll *always* be willing to help her. I mean she'll be able to come to you for *advice*.'

'Of course.' The words were little more than a grunt.

The fond mother allowed a deep sigh to escape her as she went on, 'However, I'm afraid my poor little girl is very depressed at the moment—*very* depressed indeed.'

'Really? Why would that be?' Laura asked, her voice full of sympathy.

'Because Justin hasn't been to see her,' Susan declared with frankness and in an accusing tone. 'But apart from that there's the matter of Rex's memoirs. She was so *anxious* to do them. She types *beautifully*. She does *all* our accounts on the typewriter,' she added proudly.

Justin said, 'Have you forgotten that Rochelle has already made one attempt to do them? She was unable to decipher Rex's writing—if you can call it that—

whereas Mary seems to have no difficulty at all. What's more, she's doing a really professional job. Rex is delighted with her.'

Mary glowed beneath his praise, but wisely said nothing.

However, Susan Grover did not become inarticulate, and her pale grey eyes glared at Mary as she demanded, 'How long do you intend to stay here?'

'Just until the memoirs are finished, and that should be in two or three days. Then I shall go home,' Mary told her gently.

'*Home*?' Susan snatched at the word. 'Where is home, may I ask?'

'At the moment it is Wainui Beach,' Mary replied, suddenly conscious of verbal attack from this woman.

'But—Laura told me you're an Australian,' Susan persisted.

'Yes, that's right,' Mary admitted calmly, not at all surprised to learn that she had been discussed.

Susan looked at her through narrowed lids. 'Let me guess—you're from Brisbane?'

Mary shook her head. 'No—I live in Sydney.'

'Ah—you've moved there during recent years?'

'No. I've lived in Sydney all my life.' She sent Susan Grover a direct scrutiny. 'These are strange questions, if I may say so, Mrs Grover. Have you a particular reason for asking them?'

Susan immediately backed down, then changed tack by saying, 'Laura also told me you'd been recently bereaved. So sad—so *very* sad.'

'Yes—it was my grandmother.' Mary stood up, placed her cup and saucer on the tea-trolley, then turned to Laura. 'Will you excuse me? I really must return to the office.'

Justin, who had also risen, said in a slightly mocking tone, 'I know you're anxious to leave this place, but it might not happen as soon as you hope.'

She turned surprised eyes towards him. 'What do you mean?'

'I have a suspicion that old Rex has dug up a few extra pages to be included.'

'In that case I must get back to the job.' She murmured a polite farewell to Susan Grover then left the room, closely followed by Justin. 'He hasn't said anything to me about extra pages,' she said as they walked along the passage towards the office.

'He will. Just give him time,' Justin assured her. 'I hope you won't be too upset by having to extend your time.'

'And I trust that *you* won't be too irritated by seeing me still around the place,' she flashed back at him.

'Don't talk such damned rot,' he exploded fiercely, then kicked the office door shut with a swift movement of his foot. The next moment he had taken her in his arms and, looking down into her upturned face, he spoke in firm tones. 'Now hear this—I have no wish to see you leave this place. I like having you around. You've made a difference.'

'I—I have?' she whispered, scarcely able to believe her ears.

'Yes—especially to old Rex. Laura declares he's really taken with you. His bad temper seems to have disappeared, and for this she gives you the credit.'

She gave a small shaky laugh. 'I think you'll find the answer is psychological.' She nodded towards the portrait of her grandmother. 'The likeness between myself and—and *her*—takes him back to his more youthful days, and it's possible he feels a little happier within himself. If I've made a difference to him, I'm glad,' she added softly.

'You've also made a difference to me,' he told her in a quiet voice, his hand pressing her head against his shoulder.

Contentment filled her as she continued to lean against him. 'In what way could I possibly make a difference to you?' The question came reluctantly, but she had to know.

'You've made me feel less—anti-female,' he admitted.

She giggled. 'You mean you're regaining confidence in that—kittle-cattle mob?'

'That's right. I'm beginning to realise that not all women are unreliable.'

A laugh shook her. 'Well, that's *big* of you. Indeed, *most generous*. A little more faith in the female species and you'll be brave enough to hop across the fence to collect the dowry.' She knew it was an unwise statement, but the words just came out.

He frowned, glaring down at her. 'What the hell do you mean?'

'You heard what Rochelle's mother said. Before long her daughter will own the lot. Couldn't you hear her giving you the message?'

His mouth twisted as he gritted furiously, 'If you imagine I'd marry Rochelle for a few extra acres of fruit trees, you do me a grave injustice. Is that what you really believe?'

She felt contrite. 'No—I'm sorry—I didn't mean——'

'In future kindly remember to avoid such remarks. I know Rochelle only too well. She's devious and can be quite untrustworthy. I must have honesty in a woman.'

Honesty in a woman. The words sent a pang into Mary's conscience, causing her to bite her lip as she began to disengage herself from his arms. But even as she did so they tightened about her and she found herself being pressed against him. She became vitally aware of his maleness, and of his sexual hunger that called to send tremors darting through her own body.

She tried to warn herself that it was nothing more than male hunger and quite without real depth—and then she became conscious of the intense longing building within herself. Her pulses vibrated and she gave herself up to the delicious sensations that engulfed her while his hands gently massaged the muscles along her spine.

'You don't know what you do to me,' he murmured against her lips. 'I might as well admit that your smile gets me unhinged—and as for this dimple, I long to kiss it.' He did so, then his mouth trailed across her brow and her cheeks before taking possession of her lips.

Her arms crept about his neck, and as the kiss deepened her lips parted. Her breasts were crushed against him, and as his hands gripped her buttocks to drag her even closer she felt herself drifting into a haze of ecstasy. Her heart thumped to send the blood pounding through her veins while she responded with an ardour that matched his own.

But suddenly her former thought reared its head. This was merely sexual hunger—the preliminary to his desire to make love—and to her own deep longing to give herself to him completely. In her present state of mind, and if the circumstances had been convenient, she knew she wouldn't have needed too much persuading. She knew she would not have been averse to learning the joys of lying in this man's arms. In fact, she yearned to do so.

But after that would come goodbye—and then heart-break. She would return to Sydney, never to see him again, and naturally he would forget her. And there was something else. She was afraid because she *hadn't done it before*—and as the thoughts came crowding in they were enough to bring her down from the clouds.

Her face flushed, she disengaged herself gently. 'Justin—this must stop. The memoirs are waiting.'

His eyes became intent. 'Are you saying you'd prefer to get on with them, rather than be kissed by me?'

'Of course not—but these activities could get out of hand. Besides, Mr Todd might come in.'

'Then you'd be very polite and say, "Please excuse us—Justin and I are about to make love on the hearthrug." No doubt he'd be somewhat rocked, but I'm sure he'd understand——'

'You'd expect me to be the one to tell him, especially when I've never——' The words died on her lips.

He regarded her through narrowed lids. 'Ah—I thought not. I'll just have to be patient, but, as I think I've already told you, the time will come.'

'Not if I have any say in the matter,' she told him loftily.

'Want to take a bet on it?' he queried softly.

'Certainly not.' She took a deep breath. 'Now you listen to me, Justin King. I've no intention of becoming your piece of crumpet during the remainder of my time here.' She went to the door and opened it. 'If you'll allow me to get on with the job I'll make that time as short as possible.'

'I'm requested to leave my own office?' he demanded grimly.

'That's it exactly.'

He left the room without looking at her, and she knew he was annoyed, perhaps even hurt. Then, when she eventually settled herself at the typewriter, it was several minutes before she could adjust her mind to the work in front of her. Even so another interruption was waiting to confront her, and this occurred when Rex walked into the office.

He wore a vaguely self-conscious air as he placed a handful of papers on the desk beside her, then said in a gruff voice, 'I've been thinking about what you said.'

She looked at him in silence, trying to recall what this could have been. 'Something I said?' she asked at last.

'It was that bit about the human touch,' he explained without looking at her.

She hid her surprise. 'You mean—about including family?'

'Yes.' A cough betrayed his discomfort, then he admitted, 'I told Laura what you'd said and she could see what you mean. She thinks you're quite right, and that there should be something about family in the memoirs.'

Mary looked at the extra papers lying beside her. 'These are additions which bring in Laura and Justin?'

'Well, not entirely, although of course they are mentioned.'

'But you said you had no other family.' She held her breath as she awaited his answer.

He gave another cough then mumbled, 'That wasn't the exact truth. Once—I had a daughter.'

'She died?' Mary asked in a voice that was full of sympathy.

The old man sighed. 'Only in my own mind. She insisted upon marrying a man I couldn't tolerate, so I told her to go to him and be damned. I told her to get out of my sight and never come near me again. She would have inherited this property plus a tidy nest-egg—which of course was what he had in mind—but that rat wasn't going to get his teeth into the results of my years of hard labour, so I ruined his hopes by cutting her out of my life. To me she's been dead for more than twenty years.' He sat down heavily as though exhausted by the confession.

Mary looked at him kindly. 'I think it's very sad,' she said in a low voice. 'But it is part of your life and should be included.'

'Well, it's all in these extra papers. I hope you'll be able to juggle it in somehow. Writing it down has been like lifting a load from my shoulders.'

'I'll do my best,' she promised, then looked up at the portrait. 'What about her? I hope you haven't forgotten to include her.'

'You can be sure she features in it. In fact once I began writing about family I found I couldn't stop—so I've recorded details of my parents as well as her parents, and how we met.' He paused to sigh. 'It's all so long ago.'

Mary felt a rising excitement. Now she really would learn about her roots. However, she gave no sign of her inner exhilaration as she said, 'I'm sure I'll be able to weave it in so that it reads smoothly.'

'Good girl.' He sent her a penetrating stare then asked, 'You're sure you don't mind the extra time this will take? I mean—you're not bursting to get away from this place?'

'No. I've enjoyed being at the Valencia. I'll be sorry to leave.'

'You will, huh? As far as Laura and I are concerned you can stay here for all time.'

The dimple flashed as she smiled. 'Thank you—that's very kind, but I don't think Rochelle would be pleased to see me do that. I mean—when she and Justin get married——'

His shaggy grey brows shot up. 'There's talk of it?'

'Not yet—but I understand it's what you have in mind for Justin.'

'Not any more, it isn't. I'm no longer hankering to see the two orchards combined. Never again will my wishes be forced on a living soul, and from now on I intend to mind my own damned business. I'm afraid I was unwise in my attitude towards Elizabeth.'

'You've never made any attempt to trace her—to see how she's fared?' Mary queried, recalling what Justin had told her.

'On one occasion I heard she was in Brisbane. I sent Justin to see if he could track her down. He was to observe her situation and report to me.'

'How did you expect him to find her?'

'Through various authorities. He had her name—Elizabeth Healey—and a fair indication of what she looked like,' he added, looking up at the portrait. 'But he had no luck at all.'

'Perhaps she didn't live in Brisbane,' Mary suggested.

'Well—he didn't have time to search further afield. The busy season was coming up and he had to return home. In any case, it had been only a vague hope.' He stood up and moved towards the door. 'I'll leave you to get on with it—and please believe I'm grateful for the way you've handled this job.'

After he had left the room Mary sat staring at the papers for several long moments. She had a strong urge to laugh, coupled with an urge to cry, but instead of giving way to either emotion she gathered the papers and began to decipher them.

It was all exactly as her mother had declared, and for this she was thankful because it meant that at least her grandfather had been honest. Nor had he made any attempt to excuse the hardness of his attitude. The man Healey had been an opportunist, while his daughter had been too stupidly blind to see his true colours. The old man's fury came through in definite terms, and one could only sympathise with him.

But Mother had been *young*, Mary's loyal mind defended. Nevertheless she was not so biased that she was unable to see her grandfather's side of the story, and as things had turned out he had been right. If only she could see a way of bringing them together without either being aware of manipulation, and before it was time for her parents to return to Sydney.

Later that evening the problem continued to niggle at her until at last she decided to go to bed and think about it. But as she passed the glassed front door the sight of moonlight flooding the garden caused her to pause and step out on to the veranda. The air was still and heady with the perfumed flowers of delicate white jasmine entwined round one of the pillars, and as she inhaled a deep breath of it Justin's voice spoke from behind her.

'Are you thinking of taking a walk in the moonlight? There's magic out there among the trees.'

She gave a nervous laugh. 'No—I'm not brave enough to venture out into the dark alone,' she admitted, visualising the gloom of the trees.

'You're afraid of goblins in the garden? Come with me—I'll protect you.'

She recalled the earlier moments in the office. 'You might turn out to be the biggest goblin of all.'

He looked at her intently, his eyes shadowed as he spoke gravely. 'I promise to behave. I shall keep my hands to myself unless you fall flat on your face. Then I presume it would be permissible to pick you up?'

'Only with your fingertips. I'm terrified of your arms.'

'You're saying you've no wish to feel them around you? Actually, that's not the impression I'd gathered.'

'It's just that they're so strong—and—and——'

'And you're so weak?' he finished for her.

She refused to answer, knowing that that was the situation exactly. Justin in the office was one thing—but Justin in the moonlight could be something entirely different. Not that she had the slightest intention of admitting it to him, of course.

His deep voice spoke softly. 'Shall we put it to the test? I promise to bring you back in your present state of mind—and body.' Then, without waiting for further indecision on her part, he went down the steps.

She followed him because she lacked the power to do otherwise, and when he held out his hand she took it automatically, nor was she unaware of the firm grip of his fingers.

They walked in a companionable silence while she searched in her mind for normal conversation, and eventually she said, 'You were perfectly right when you said Mr Todd would come to light with additions to the memoirs. They're really quite a surprise——'

He cut her short. 'This is not the moment to be discussing memoirs. These are *our* moments. Tell me more about yourself and your bright Sydney life.'

She laughed. 'What bright Sydney life?'

'Don't tell me it isn't one round of gaiety—a far cry from life on a quiet orchard several miles out of

Gisborne. Even Gisborne itself is isolated from other cities by miles of hill country.'

'I'm sorry if I've appeared bored,' she said quietly.

'Ah—but that's only because you've been kept busy.'

'Does Rochelle suffer from boredom?' she queried in a sweet tone.

'I doubt it—but that's because she has the interest of the orchard she'll own sooner or later.'

'Of course—the *dowry*.' Then she went on hastily, 'If I loved a man who owned an orchard I could become as interested as Rochelle because I'd want to work beside him. Or do you consider I'm too scatty to do so?' she flashed at him, fearing this to be the case.

As she spoke her foot went into an uneven piece of ground, causing her to stumble. His hand shot out to grab her arm and drag her against him, and as she leaned on him she felt the firm beat of his heart.

'I said you'd fall flat on your face,' he reminded her mockingly.

A shaky laugh escaped her. 'I'm not wearing the best of shoes for moonlight walking in long grass.'

He looked down into her upturned face. 'I intend to claim a reward for saving your fall.' He kissed her briefly, then put her away from him, his hands firm as he placed her at arm's length. 'There now—does that feel safer?' he teased.

She made no reply, but was more than conscious of her own deep disappointment. Here they were—out in the moonlight and without fear of being observed—and she knew she wanted to be kissed. But, recalling their conversation on the veranda, she supposed it was her own fault that he made no attempt to hold her close to him. But of course if he had really wanted to do so, nothing would have stopped him.

This last thought caused a depression she found difficult to shake off, and she could find little to say as he led her beyond the oranges towards the boundary fence. They were now on a firmer track that led towards the back of the garages with their iron roofs shining in the moonlight. Beyond the garages she knew that the track would branch and lead away to the right towards the fertiliser shed where Justin kept records of his Valencia Mix.

Straining her eyes, she could barely see it nestling in the gloom of its sheltering trees, but even as she stared in its direction she imagined she saw a light flash across its one small high window. Or was it a gleam of moonlight? She stood still, waiting for it to happen again.

Justin turned to look at her. 'Is something the matter?'

Her voice became a whisper as she gripped his arm. 'I thought I saw a light. Could anyone be in the fertiliser shed?'

'At this time of night? You've got to be joking.'

'Perhaps Mr Todd has gone there for some reason.'

'Rex? He's dead to the world in front of the TV.'

'Well, I only saw a flash. I suppose anyone going there would switch on the light.'

'That's most unlikely, for the simple reason that there's no power connected to the shed. It's not a place one uses at night. You probably saw moonlight on the window.'

'Then why isn't it there now? Justin—I feel sure I saw a light.' Mary remained rooted to the spot, staring in the direction of the shed. The light flashed again and she was triumphant. 'There—I told you so.'

An oath escaped him, then he muttered, 'Who the hell——?' and began to stride forward.

She raced to grip his arm. 'Justin—be careful. Wouldn't it be wiser to approach quietly?' she whispered urgently.

'Of course—you're right,' he agreed in a low voice.

They walked rapidly and without noise towards the shed. As they approached the small building he signalled for her to remain at a distance, but she shook her head and followed closely behind him.

The door of the shed was ajar, but inside a dim light could be seen and the figure of a person who held a torch while writing on a pad which rested on the bench. Notes from Justin's records were being copied.

Justin pushed the door open. 'Well, well, well,' he exclaimed, stepping into the shed. 'Have you been able to find all you want?' His voice was heavy with sarcasm.

The figure swung round to face him. It was Rochelle.

CHAPTER SEVEN

ROCHELLE gaped at them, then immediately regained her composure. 'Justin—I'm so glad you've come at last!' she exclaimed.

'What the devil are you doing here?' he gritted furiously.

The pale grey eyes widened. 'Why—waiting for you, of course. You said to meet you here at nine o'clock and you'd give me your special orange-tree formula.'

'At such a late hour? You must be raving,' he snarled.

'No, I'm not. Surely you remember. I got tired of waiting so I decided to find it for myself.'

He frowned, staring at her. 'When—may I ask—did I arrange to meet you here?'

'Oh—a few days ago,' she asserted stubbornly. 'It was after I'd given you my wonderful news.'

'News? What news?' he demanded. 'What are you talking about?'

'The news of Daddy's intentions about putting the orchard in my name. Don't you remember? I was telling you about it when she came looking for marmalade fruit.' Rochelle sent an angry glare towards Mary. '*Marmalade fruit*,' she repeated sneeringly. 'She could see we were talking together and it was just a ploy to interrupt us. She should've backed off.'

As Mary listened to the tirade directed against herself she recalled her grandfather saying that Rochelle had come to Justin with news.

Justin said, 'I remember you told me about the orchard arrangements, but I have no recollection of making an appointment to meet you here, especially at this hour. Nor would I divulge the results of my experiments before

I was entirely satisfied with them, and, as you yourself must realise, that would take several seasons.'

Rochelle faced him defiantly. 'Then, if you made no arrangements to meet me, what has brought you here now?' she demanded with a hint of triumph.

He merely looked at her in silence.

Rochelle pressed home the vantage. 'You *see*—you *did* arrange to meet me here. It's just that you're late. But what's *she* doing here? Couldn't you get rid of her?' Her voice had risen.

'Take it easy, Rochelle—you're becoming hysterical,' Justin admonished calmly. 'Mary and I were taking a moonlight stroll. She saw the light flash on the window, therefore we came to investigate.'

Rochelle took a deep breath as she hissed, 'You stood me up to go moonlight walking with *her*? *I'll get her for this*.'

'Don't talk like an idiot,' Justin snapped. 'Do you want Mary to report your threats to the police? She has a witness, you know.'

Rochelle laughed. 'You wouldn't go against me——'

'Wouldn't I? Don't count on it,' he rasped, then went to the bench to lift the torch, which was still switched on. He played the beam round the shed's interior, then it rested on the open sack of Valencia Mix. From there it moved to a small plastic bag which sat on the bench beside Rochelle's pad and the open record book.

He snatched up the bag, then turned on her with renewed fury. 'So you're not only copying records, you're also taking a sample for analysis. This is blatant thievery, Rochelle.'

'It is not!' she shrieked. 'You *promised* to give me the formula.'

'*I did not*,' he rasped, then tore the page from her pad. 'Now get out of this shed and take yourself home. In future the door will be padlocked. The bar across the outside is obviously not enough.'

Rochelle sent a baleful glare towards Mary, then left without further argument.

'I told you she was devious,' Justin murmured as he closed the door and set the outside bar in place to keep it shut.

Mary hesitated then asked, 'Are you sure you haven't forgotten you made these promises? She seemed so positive about it.'

'Of course I'm sure.' The moonlight revealed his expression of fury. 'Now you know what I mean by kittle cattle. Women are not to be trusted.' He strode towards the house, causing Mary to run to keep up with his pace.

His words made her feel miserable. It was as though Rochelle's actions reflected upon herself—and that she too had sunk beyond the pale. And this is exactly what would happen if—or when—he learnt more about herself.

They returned to the house in an almost unbroken silence. The moonlight walk had been a disaster.

A few mornings later Justin walked into the office. He wore an expensive green sports jacket over darker green trousers, giving the appearance that he had something other than work in mind. He looked at the pile of neatly typed pages, lifted the top one and began to scan the lines. 'How much more is there to do?' he asked.

'Not much. I'm almost at the end.' She straightened her back and stretched her arms, at the same time reaching to flick the page from his fingers. 'You may read it when Mr Todd gives you permission,' she said in firm tones while returning it to the pile.

'A mass of confessions, is it?'

She smiled. 'There are a few in the extra pages. When I've finished juggling them into the right places you'll be able to return me to Wainui Beach.'

'That'll be a relief.'

'You mean to yourself, of course. Thank you very much. There's no need to rub it in.'

'Must you take it the wrong way? I meant it would be a relief to you. Your trip to New Zealand has been nothing but work.'

She hesitated, then admitted, 'I've spoken to Mother on the phone. She said they're ready to leave Gisborne and are now filling in time by having a holiday. Father is taking her round all his old boyhood haunts.'

'While you've seen nothing of the district.'

'At least I was taken to see the view from Kaiti Hill. Thank you for that.'

'That's why I've come to see you now. I need to take a run sixty miles south to Wairoa. You're coming with me.'

'This is an order from the orchard king himself?'

'You may look upon it as such,' he grinned.

Her lips tightened as she sent him a level glance. 'Wouldn't it be more preferable for this member of the kittle-cattle mob to finish the job so that she can remove her obnoxious female presence from your stronghold— and your sight?'

'Sarcasm doesn't suit you. In any case I no longer consider you to be in that category.'

'Ah—but you did.'

'That was before the days of my enlightenment. I now suggest that not all women are alike.' His tone altered to a softer note. 'Nor is this really an order. It's a plea from one who would enjoy your company.'

His words filled her with a surge of pleasure that was difficult to conceal. 'Thank you. Is it a business trip?'

'Not exactly. Ella has a cousin living in Wairoa. I'm hoping to employ him as a handyman and gardener. Our last man left a short time before you arrived. We'll leave as soon as you're ready to tear yourself away from that typewriter.'

She stood up. 'Just give me a few minutes to powder my nose.' Then, as she hurried to her room, she was gripped by intense excitement. She was going out with Justin. They'd be together for *hours*. Make the most of it, she told herself. Enjoy this day which will be the first and last of its kind.

A vigorous brushing to her dark hair made it shine and curl about her face. Her make-up received careful attention, and as she snatched up a matching jacket to her blue full skirt with its blue and white top she paused to examine her reflection in the long mirror of the wardrobe. It was then she realised that her eyes were shining, and that she'd be unwise to expect too much of this day.

She left the bedroom, and as she walked along the passage she presumed he'd be waiting for her in the living-room, but he was not there. Nor was he in the car, which stood parked at the front door. She then hurried back to the office, where she found him reading one of her recently typed pages while holding several others in his hand.

From the doorway she protested, 'I *told* you—you're not supposed to be reading it yet.'

His face had become grim. 'Why not? I'd see it sooner or later.' He tapped the page. 'I'm finding this part of it to be most interesting. So the daughter didn't desert him after all.'

Mary sent him a rueful smile. 'I never did believe that part of your story.'

'He didn't tell me he'd thrown her out—that he'd told her to go to hell and never show her face again.'

'I suppose not. Personally I think it's a miracle he's admitting it now.' She took the papers from him and laid them on the pile.

He eyed her narrowly. 'What made you so sure the desertion story was wrong? It's what he'd said, so why should you doubt it?'

She opened her mouth to speak, then closed it again. Now was not the time for revelations. They'd be sure to ruin the day, therefore she raked in her mind then glanced up at the portrait. 'Does that woman look as though she'd desert anyone?' she asked quietly.

He followed her gaze. 'No—not really.'

'Then I don't believe her daughter would do so either.' She moved towards the door. 'Shall we go?'

A short time later they were on the highway leading south. A feeling of peace stole over Mary as she relaxed against the seat, its cause lying in the fact that Justin was now aware of the truth—or at least part of it—and that he no longer believed the desertion story. It was a good feeling, and a sigh of contentment escaped her.

He glanced at her, a faint smile playing about his lips. 'I hope you're comfortable?'

She sent him a radiant smile. 'Wonderfully so, thank you, and loving every minute of this drive. The country is so lush and green. I've never seen so many ewes, lambs and cows to each field.'

'Steers—not cows,' he corrected with a grin. 'You must remember this is springtime, when the pastures need to be controlled. The cattle eat the long grass to enable the sheep to nibble the sweet short grass that comes away so quickly.'

She said, 'It's so different from Australia. Over there we'd be driving through endless stretches of gum trees——'

'With the odd kangaroo hopping across the road——'

'But here the hills are so close, and so high.'

As the highway twisted and turned up a long grade he said, 'This is the Wharerata Hill, which rises to more than sixteen hundred feet. There's a viewpoint at the top.' A few minutes later, as they reached the summit, he pulled into the parking area.

The panorama was breath-taking, and as she looked eastward beyond the foreground of jagged hill-tops that descended to the coast she felt his chin rest against her head.

His deep voice spoke near her ear. 'Do you see Gisborne in the distance? And that long headland is the southern side of Young Nick's Head.'

'It's—it's a terrific view,' she agreed shakily, the feel of his chin taking precedence over what she could see.

'Now look this way.' His arm encircling her shoulder drew her round to face the opposite direction, and she then gazed towards countless ranges that lay in uneven tiers until they disappeared into dark clouds edging the western sky.

Justin did not follow her gaze. Instead, his finger traced a line down her cheek. 'Are you aware that you have a lovely face?' he asked quietly.

His words sent warmth through her body. 'You're supposed to be looking at the view,' she reminded him firmly.

'I've seen it many times.'

'Then look again and tell me if those horrible clouds over the ranges mean rain.'

'Not before we return home. I've ordered a perfect day just for us—one that will remain sunny and last in our memories.' His eyes had become intent as they continued to rest on her features.

'For all time.' The words slipped out impulsively.

'Amen to that,' he said in a grave tone, then kissed the dimple that had flashed in her cheek.

She leaned back in her seat. 'Aren't we supposed to be on our way to Wairoa?' Her eyes strayed westward again.

'We'll get there in good time. Why are you looking so serious?'

'I find the purple-blackness of those clouds ominous. They're like an omen of evil creeping up on a day that is so blissfully sunny.' The words ended with a small shudder.

'You're being fanciful,' Justin remarked, sending her a sharp glance. 'What put such a depressing thought into your head?'

'Perhaps I'm enjoying the day too much. I'd hate anything to ruin it,' she admitted, wondering why the clouds had affected her in this stupid manner.

He stared straight ahead as he said, 'Is that a hint for me to keep my hands to myself? I may look, but I mustn't touch?'

Mary ignored both questions while searching for an explanation that would satisfy her own mind. 'I've always hated black clouds,' she admitted. 'Perhaps it's a hangover from my childhood, when I was afraid of the dark.'

'I'll bet you went to bed with a nightlight,' he teased.

'Yes, I did. But I've grown out of those childish habits.'

He sent her a side glance. 'You don't sound very convincing—especially with dark clouds hovering over the horizon.'

They had been driving for almost an hour when they reached an area that brought an exclamation from Mary. 'This is an attractive place!' she said, looking at the stream that rippled and sparkled beside extensive camping facilities.

'It's the Morere Hot Springs Reserve,' Justin informed her.

She gazed up at a hilly patchwork of different shades of green, then asked, 'Is that native bush?'

'Yes. The Reserve covers five hundred acres. It's difficult to believe that most of this east coast land was once covered in similar bush.'

'But where are the hot springs?'

'You walk up through the bush to them. Would you like to stop and do so on the way home?'

Her eyes shone. 'Oh, yes, that would be lovely—an added bonus to this drive.'

Another twenty-five miles took them to Wairoa, where the main shopping area was situated along the bank of a wide, slowly flowing river. Justin took her to lunch in a restaurant overlooking the riverbank, where people sat on seats or spread rugs on the grass while eating sandwiches. Her previous brief gloom caused by the thought of darkness had now left her, and she was filled with contentment just to be with him.

Later they crossed the river bridge in search of the boarding-house where Ella's cousin lived. He was a small, wiry man, who came out to the car, and, listening to his thanks, Mary sensed that he was truly grateful for the offer made by Justin. Nor was he unappreciative when Justin gave him the money for his fare to Gisborne.

As they left him standing on the footpath Justin said, 'He's been made redundant because of his age, but he's not too old to see to the firewood and gardening at Valencia. Ella's been worried about him. She told me where to find George Brody.'

Mary was suddenly filled with a new respect for the man sitting beside her. He feels for people, she realised as they drove over the bridge again. He's ready to hold out a helping hand. And then she became aware that he had not turned towards the hill that would take them out of Wairoa. Instead, he was driving through streets that were taking them to higher ground at the town's southern end.

Minutes later they stopped at the front entrance of an extensive sprawl of buildings, and she realised they were at the Public Hospital. I might have known, she thought, watching him get out and open the boot to extract bags of oranges, lemons and tangelos. She left her seat and helped to carry them in, and it was while doing so that she realised she loved him. The knowledge left her feeling stunned, and she stood with a bag of lemons in her hand, her eyes wide, her jaw sagging slightly.

He came to her side, his expression one of concern. 'Are you all right?' he asked, taking the lemons from her.

She gulped and was afraid to look at him. 'Yes—I'm OK——'

'Then why are you looking like a stuffed owl? You appear to be riveted to the spot.'

'Thank you for the kind words,' she said bleakly.

'You know I didn't mean to be uncomplimentary—but you're gawping as if you've just had a shock.'

'It was something that—that just hit me,' she admitted. 'It's entirely private,' she declared firmly when he appeared to be ready to pursue the matter.

'Well, so long as you're not stricken with something that forces me to leave you here,' he said, still eyeing her anxiously.

'Of course not. I'm quite all right.'

'OK—we'll head for home.'

Had he forgotten about the promised bush walk at Morere? she wondered. He'd made no further mention of it, and she vowed to say nothing to remind him. However, her fears were groundless because he slackened speed as they ran beside a stream, then turned into the Reserve's parking area.

He opened the door for her, then locked the car. His hand on her arm drew her towards the track leading into the bush, where their feet made no sound on a path that was soft with leaf mould. It was like stepping into another world where everything was still, except for the flash of wings from a nearby bird.

In places the afternoon sun sent golden shafts through the high arched fronds topping the black trunks of tree ferns, and it gleamed on the long, stiff, upright leaves of nikau palms. They walked beside a stream that bubbled over a narrow bed, and everywhere there were small ferns to cover banks or dip fronds in the water.

'It's a place of dreams,' Mary said while looking up at some of the larger trees and wondering how old they were. She was also vitally aware that Justin was holding her hand, but she did not withdraw it because his touch was all part of the magic of being here.

He led her along various paths that wound on an upward grade until eventually they reached the hot thermal pools with their changing facilities and showers. Seats offered a welcome rest after the walk, and as they sat on a bench Justin told her about the various pools, which ranged in heat from thirty-two to forty degrees Celsius.

'They were discovered in 1884 by Europeans who pushed through the bush to investigate what appeared to be smoke from a fire, but of course it was steam from the pools——'

His words were interrupted by the sound of rich, bell-like chimes that carolled on the still air. 'That's a tui,' he said, looking about him for the feathered songster. 'Ah—there it is. It's a honey-eater and is also known as the parson-bird because of its white cravat. It sings before dawn, and doesn't stop until after dusk.'

Mary followed his gaze to where a shaft of sunlight gave bluish and greenish glows to the bird's black plumage, and highlighted a curving tuft of white feathers that hung from its throat. 'Its notes have the tone of a melodious grandfather clock,' she said, then left the seat to move closer to the bird, which was perched on a fairly low branch of a tree with moss-covered trunk and limbs.

Bright eyes watched her slow step-by-step approach, but even as she paused to stand perfectly still the tui fluttered and hopped from bough to bough until it was in a tree a short distance from the track. She tried to follow its progress, stepping carefully over twigs and fallen nikau palm fronds that lay on the soft spongy ground.

'Watch your step,' Justin warned from where he sat. 'I can hear him laughing at you.'

But she took no heed as, fascinated, she followed the bird deeper into the bush. Then, with her eyes lifted upwards, she failed to see a protruding root that sent her sprawling while the tui flashed away, its wings echoing the swish of taffeta.

Justin was beside her in an instant, lifting her in strong arms that carried her back to the seat. He brushed her free of leaf mould and moss, then lifted twigs from her hair. 'One keeps to the track in the New Zealand bush,' he warned gravely.

She stood and looked up at him sheepishly. 'Thank you for picking me up,' she said in a small meek voice.

'I'm afraid I had to use my arms—rather than fingertips,' he said in a dry tone. 'I recall you said you were afraid of my arms. I can't help wondering why that would be.'

She looked down to avoid his steady gaze. 'It's because they hold me so closely,' she admitted while a flush rose to her cheeks.

'And that is most distasteful to you?' The dark grey eyes were watching her intently, almost as though burrowing into her mind to get at the truth. 'Please be honest about it.'

'No—of course it's not distasteful.' The words came in a whisper, but she was still unable to look at him.

'In that case, after the *ghastly* ordeal of being almost buried alive beneath several tons of leaves, you might like to be kissed better?'

She gave a nervous laugh, then, because she loved him and hadn't the power to resist him, she raised her face and said, 'Yes, please——'

He snatched her against his body, his arms almost crushing the breath out of her while his lips found her mouth with a surge of passion he made no attempt to conceal.

She closed her eyes and responded, her arms creeping about his neck as throbs of happiness swept through her entire being. At the same time she knew she must be careful, because in her present state of mind it would be all too easy to betray her love for him.

She was also aware that they could be observed in this close embrace, but for some strange reason it didn't seem to matter. A similar opportunity to be held in his arms might not come again before she left the Valencia, therefore she must not deny herself these few precious moments.

Instinct then warned that she was being a fool to allow her emotions to get so completely out of control—yet she seemed to be unable to do anything about it. And then these blissful moments were blown apart by the sound of voices coming from further along the track that continued to wind through the bush.

Justin put her from him with a few whispered words. 'Later, my love—later.'

Her eyes held questions but he said nothing more as they retraced their steps back to the car.

He opened the door for her, then leaned over to fasten her seatbelt. In adjusting its position his hand lingered on her breast while his fingers caressed her erect nipple. His lips brushed her own, then he looked deeply into her eyes for several long moments before closing the door and walking round the car to take his seat behind the wheel.

Mary sat in a daze as they drove towards home. 'Later, my love,' he'd said. Did this mean that later that evening they'd make love? Was this his way of saying he *loved* her?

He cut into her thoughts to say casually, 'Before you leave we could come back and do one of the longer bush walks. The Ridge Track is fairly easy walking, but it takes two hours, while the Mangakawa Track is a more strenuous effort that takes at least three hours. Of course you'll need to wear suitable shoes.'

Before you leave. His words brought Mary down to earth with a shock. Well, there was her answer. Justin was obviously having no difficulty in mastering his own emotions, she thought sadly. Oh, yes, his desires came through clearly enough, but wasn't that just his male hunger—his *need*—for sex? There'd be no depth to it because he had no *real* love for her. His use of the word had been merely a casual endearment.

If he'd had any sincere feelings for her he'd have given a hint of it—wouldn't he? she reasoned, her thoughts becoming more depressed with every passing mile. And when she left the orchard he'd forget her within a short time. Freedom was what he had in mind, while she herself had been crazy enough to have allowed him to creep into her heart.

'You've become very quiet,' he remarked, sending her a side glance. 'Are you becoming bored with this outing?'

'How could you possibly ask such a question?' she exclaimed, then, searching for an excuse to cover her ponderings, she explained, 'It's just that I feel I've spent so much time away from the memoirs, I'll have to make up for it this evening.'

He laughed. 'So that anyone who imagines he'll have his way with you tonight will discover you to be *very busy*?'

She bit her lip, realising he could read her like a book, but she went on defensively, 'Mr Todd is not paying me to take trips to Wairoa—or to walk in the bush——'

'Or to spend time in my arms,' he added softly.

And to those words she could find no reply, therefore she sat in silence while savouring the recollection of those precious moments. However, when they reached home they discovered that friends of Justin's had phoned to say they would visit him that evening. It meant that any plans he might have had for spending time alone with Mary were thwarted, and she was unsure whether to be relieved or bitterly disappointed.

Nor would Justin allow her to disappear into the office to make up time lost during the day. 'Bill is my oldest and best friend,' he explained in an aggrieved tone. 'He and Jean are on their honeymoon. I'm sure she'd appreciate another woman to talk to.'

'Won't Laura be there?' Mary asked with a hint of surprise.

'Laura and Rex like to go to bed early, but if you're there Laura won't feel obliged to stay up. You'll like Jean. She's only a year or so older than yourself. Bill's been itching to get married for ages,' he added.

'Unlike his friend, Justin,' Mary commented with a smile.

He ignored the remark. 'Please forget the memoirs for this evening. I want you to meet Jean—and I want Jean to meet you.'

Again she was surprised. 'Why would that be?'

'Because you both come from Sydney,' he explained. 'So will you help me make their evening a pleasant one?'

She knew she'd be ungracious to refuse, therefore she said, 'Yes—if you really want me to do so.'

'Thank you. Laura says she's invited them to come for the evening meal so I'll have a quick shower and shave.'

Mary also decided to shower and change into another dress, and when she appeared in the living-room she was wearing a fine woollen dress of deep violet. It enhanced her clear complexion and made her eyes look like purple pansies.

Rex looked at her with admiration as he said, 'That dress is really quite stylish, although I must admit I like you best in blue.'

There was a hint of grumpiness in his tone that made her smile inwardly, but her face remained serious. 'Blue isn't the only colour a girl likes to wear,' she said gently.

Justin made an unexpected remark. 'I'm waiting to see her in white—something lacy and frothy—and with a veil.'

His words caused her heart to leap as she turned to look at him. 'What on earth are you talking about?' she asked, remaining calm only with an effort.

Laura became alert. 'It sounds like a wedding dress,' she said, her eyes darting from Mary to Justin.

Justin spoke in a bland manner. 'Naturally, Mary will get married sooner or later—and I expect to be invited to the wedding.'

Mary turned to face him. Was he trying to tell her something? she wondered. A message such as, some day you'll get married—but not to me? I shall be a guest—nothing more, nothing less?

Her face remained serious as she said, 'You've no need to be concerned, Justin. I've got the message.'

Rex grumbled crossly, 'Why must you young people talk in riddles?'

But before anyone could think of an answer the front door-chimes echoed through the house. Justin left the room and moments later he returned with two people whose affectionate attitude towards each other soon betrayed their newly married status. Introductions were made, and they looked at Mary with interest. Then, perhaps because of their own happiness, Bill and Jean Stanton immediately assumed that Mary was Justin's fiancée.

'Met your match at last, old chap?' Bill exclaimed heartily.

Mary turned crimson then said hastily, 'No—you're mistaken. Justin's fiancée lives next door——' She stopped, wondering what had made her make such a statement, and aware that Justin was looking at her with an angry expression on his face. Then she went on in a voice that was not quite steady, 'Actually, I live in Sydney. I'll be going home quite soon.'

'*Sydney*!' Jean echoed. 'That's my home town.'

It was enough to draw the two girls together, and for the rest of the evening they chatted with the companionship of friends who had known each other for years. On the other side of the room Justin and Bill talked over old times, while Laura and Rex remained only until they could politely excuse themselves and retire for the night.

Mary hardly noticed their departure. But what she *did* notice was that Justin scarcely spoke to her, or even looked in her direction during the evening, and she sensed that he was more annoyed with her than she'd realised.

Why, oh, *why* had she made that *stupid* remark about his fiancée being next door? And then the answer shot into her mind with piercing clarity. She was jealous, of course—jealous of Rochelle, who would remain so near

to Justin while she herself would be so far away. She
was jealous of Rochelle who could dangle a dowry before
his nose.

She tried to push the thoughts away while talking to
Jean about Sydney places they both knew, but as the
evening wore on Justin's silence towards herself became
even more noticeable, so that it was a relief when it
became time for the visitors to leave. Then, as he stood
on the veranda watching their car disappear, she hurried
into her bedroom before his wrath could descend upon
her.

By morning he'd have got over his fit of pique, because surely it was no more than that, she assured herself
while cleaning her teeth and removing make-up. Nor
would she see him at breakfast, she thought as she pulled
a flimsy nightdress over her head. He'd been away for
most of today, therefore he'd be in the packing shed or
out in the orchard at an early hour.

But Mary was mistaken in thinking she could avoid
hearing what Justin had to say to her, and she hadn't
been in bed long before she heard the movement of a
door-latch. Was somebody trying to enter her room?
Startled, she sat up and looked at the door leading into
the passage, but there was no movement from it. Then
she realised it was the door leading out on to the veranda.

Her heart leapt to her throat as she recalled that in
her haste to get into bed and switch off the light she'd
forgotten to check that it was locked.

She watched, wide-eyed, the blankets pulled high
under her chin, as the door opened slowly. Moonlight
illuminated the room, sending beams from a high
window to enable her to see the figure of a man, then
her fears left her as she saw it was Justin.

He strode to the bedside and switched on the table
lamp, then stood staring at her. His dark brows were
drawn together, his mouth was an angry line. When he
spoke his words were clipped.

'I thought you'd have had the grace to explain yourself before skipping off to bed at break-neck speed.'

'Wh-what do you mean?' she prevaricated.

'You know damned well that I mean the fact of your telling Bill and Jean that my *fiancée* lives next door. It's a wonder you didn't go into details concerning the *dowry*. So—would you kindly explain why you made that statement?'

Mary crouched down in the bed, still gripping the blankets.

'I'm waiting to hear your reasons,' he gritted.

She licked dry lips while trying to find words.

He seated himself on the side of the bed. 'You'll tell me—even if it takes all night to drag it out of you.'

CHAPTER EIGHT

JUSTIN continued to glare at her. 'I'm waiting,' he said grimly.

Mary returned his glare. 'If you don't get out of this room I'll start yelling,' she warned in the coldest voice she could muster. 'Mr Todd will be coming at the gallop.'

Justin was amused. 'I think he's past his galloping days,' he drawled. 'So what shall you tell him when he does totter in? That you're being raped?'

'I doubt that he'd believe me,' she said morosely.

'Or he might tell you to shut up and get on with it—and to stop disturbing his sleep.'

She looked at him in silence, her eyes reflecting her misery.

He went on in a softer tone, 'I thought I'd made it perfectly clear that I'll never marry Rochelle. She tells lies. I'd never know whether or not I could believe her. I've got a thing about deceit. I hate it.'

Her misery deepened, knowing that when he learned the truth about herself he'd despise her. And while she longed to tell him of her relationship to Rex Todd she felt that now was not the right moment to do so.

Perhaps—with luck—she'd finish the memoirs tomorrow or the next day, and as soon as they'd been approved by her grandfather she'd admit her identity and then ask Justin to drive her home to Wainui Beach. No doubt it would be the last she'd ever see of him.

His voice cut into her ponderings. 'I could've sworn you had enjoyed yourself today,' he pursued relentlessly.

She sat up, still gripping the bedding beneath her chin. 'I did—oh, I *did*. I loved every minute of it. How can you think otherwise?'

His jaw tightened. 'Because I've been given reason to doubt it.'

'How can you say that?' she quavered.

'Because you ruined the day without giving it so much as a second thought. You made that ludicrous statement about Rochelle being my fiancée. After our moments of closeness at Morere it made me feel positively sick to realise you could be so sure I'd double-cross her.'

The knowledge of how badly she had hurt him caused Mary's eyes to fill with tears, and in a moment of desperation she forgot about the scantiness of her nightdress top. Her hands went out to clasp his arm, causing the blankets to slip down to a lower and more revealing level. 'I'm sorry, Justin—really, I'm sorry,' she said in a voice filled with remorse. Then, because she was unable to control her tongue, the admission bubbled forth. 'If you must know the truth, I was jealous—jealous of the thought of you holding her——'

He looked at her incredulously, his voice softening. '*Jealous*? Of Rochelle? You really mean it?'

She nodded, looking at him with eyes which were so tear-filled that they appeared to be blue pools.

His brow cleared. 'In that case—all is forgiven.' He reached to draw her against him, one arm enfolding her while the fingers of his other hand became laced in her hair.

She clung to him with a sigh of relief. 'I hated the thought of quarrelling with you on what could be one of my last nights here.'

'You're so near the end?' he asked, his cheek against her head.

'Yes. The manuscript is almost ready for Mr Todd's final approval, and then it will go to the printer.'

'What about proof-reading?'

She shook her head gently. 'I doubt that I'll be here to do that.'

Justin made no reply as his mouth traced a line across her brow, then descended to her cheeks. His arms

tightened about her, his lips finding her own with almost
brutal force.

She responded in a daze of happiness, her arms entwined about his neck while her heart thumped wildly.
At any moment now he would tell her he loved her, she
thought. He couldn't possibly kiss her like this without
loving her, and, feeling so sure about this, she made no
protest when her shoulder-straps were slipped down to
enable him to kiss her breasts.

The feel of his tongue on her nipples sent wild sensations coursing through her entire body, forcing it to
throb with a yearning desire that left her gasping. She
longed to plead with him to take her—and to make
love—then she gasped when he pushed the bedding away
and lay beside her, crushing her against his arousal.

Soft whisperings of endearments came to her ears, then
ceased abruptly as he kissed her deeply. As it ended there
was a moment's silence between them before he said,
'You see what you do to me? You've almost made me
lose control.'

She sighed, knowing that she longed for him to lose
control, then his next movements caused her heart to
sink.

Gently and firmly he removed her arms from about
his neck, then he left her to stand beside the bed. An
abrupt movement jerked the bedclothes into place.
'Goodnight,' he muttered. 'Go to sleep.'

It was almost as if he had rejected her, and she lay
gripped by a feeling of anticlimax as he left the room.
'Go to sleep,' he'd said. How could she possibly go to
sleep? Nor had he said he loved her. Obviously he didn't.
It was then that the tears began to soak into the pillow.

Next morning she was at the desk at an early hour,
determined to finish the task and to get away as soon as
possible. It was strange, she thought. Not so long ago
she had been most anxious to come to the Valencia—
but now she couldn't be more anxious to leave.

Nor did she see Justin during the morning, and for this she was thankful, mainly because she was unsure of how she could face him after her uninhibited performance of allowing him to kiss her breasts. Even the memory brought colour to her cheeks and made her feel hot all over.

However, she did see her grandfather when the old man came in carrying a box of photographs. The sight of it startled her, but she immediately hid her dismay.

He placed it on Justin's desk. 'I think I mentioned there'd be photos,' he remarked casually while beginning to shuffle through them. 'I'm afraid some of them are rather old.'

'Yes—you did. But I've been so engrossed with the script I'd forgotten about them.' Here was more delay, she thought, frustrated.

'We'll have to go through the box to find the ones that will reproduce best,' he said.

'And then the captions must be attended to,' she pointed out while making an effort to sound nonchalant about the extra work.

He handed a photo to her. 'That's Elizabeth—the daughter I told you about. It was taken on her twenty-first birthday.'

Mary stared at it in silence, amazed by the likeness to herself. And then she sensed that Rex Todd was watching her closely. Did he suspect? she wondered. Should she admit to their relationship now and get it off her chest? No. Instinct warned that with this unforeseen work of illustrations she'd be wiser to wait just a little longer, or until she was about to leave as she'd previously decided.

At that moment Ella came to the office door. 'Lunch is ready when you are,' she told Rex. 'Justin is pouring sherries—and we have a guest,' she added in a resigned tone while a pained expression crossed her face.

'I'll wash my hands,' Mary said, leaving the typewriter, then hurried to her room where she also smoothed more colour to her lips and ran a comb through her hair.

These actions were not because of the guest, but for Justin, and somehow they seemed to give her more confidence to face him. But when she entered the living-room she found herself confronted by Rochelle.

At the sight of Mary, Rochelle's pale grey eyes widened. 'Good grief—*you're* still here?' The words were followed by a silence, which caused her to look at the others and say, 'I'm only joking—of course I *knew* she was here. I saw her in the orchard yesterday afternoon.'

Justin said, 'That was when we were at Morere. Let me congratulate you on your eyesight, Rochelle.'

Rochelle pouted. 'Oh—well, it must've been somebody else. One of the pickers, perhaps.' Her eyes flashed a look from Justin to Mary, where they remained accusingly. '*Morere*, huh?'

Mary had no wish to follow the subject of Morere, therefore she forced a smile and said, 'As it happens the job would've been finished if extra material hadn't come up, and now there are photos for illustrations to be chosen.'

Rex spoke to Rochelle. 'What brings you here, young lady?' he demanded bluntly. 'You don't usually visit us at this hour of the day. Is your father needing help from Justin?'

She laughed. 'Oh, no—nothing like that. Daddy is *very* self-sufficient, as you know. We have *everything* we need.' She sent him a dazzling smile while pushing strands of long blonde hair from her face. 'I happened to be passing your entrance when my conscience hit me with a mighty big bang.'

Rex eyed her searchingly. 'This sounds interesting,' he said.

'So I turned round and drove in. I explained to Laura that I *must* apologise to Justin—and she kindly invited me to do so over lunch.'

'I really don't know what you're talking about,' Justin said from across the room as he handed a sherry to Mary.

'Give her time,' Mary whispered.

Justin eyed her critically. 'As for you, you have shadows under your eyes. Are you feeling OK?'

She looked away from him. 'Of course. Bright as a spark.'

Rochelle continued, 'Naturally, I could've *phoned* to apologise, but I preferred to do it *personally*.'

'So what's it all about?' Rex demanded impatiently.

'You can tell us during lunch. Ella has just taken the trolley through to the dining-room, so please come and bring your sherries with you,' Laura said, leading the way.

'And about time too,' Rex growled.

As they left the living-room Mary whispered to Justin, 'Do you think it's about the fertiliser shed incident? Instead of waiting to apologise when you're alone, she's making a thing of it, which I find rather strange—unless she has a reason for all this hooey.'

He smiled. 'Haven't you realised, she's a strange girl?'

When they were all seated at the table Rex's curiosity got the better of him. He looked at Rochelle from beneath his grey brows and said, 'Well, young lady—what's all this business about an apology?'

She took a deep breath and looked round the table before she said, 'Actually, it began one night recently when Mother said she must go to the supermarket in Gisborne the next day. I said I'd go with her, and then Daddy said I'd better bring home some bags of fertiliser.' She turned to smile at Rex. 'I suppose you do know that Daddy is transferring the orchard into my name?'

Rex looked sceptical then grunted, 'I did hear something about it. I presume he's gone into what it'll cost him in gift duty?'

Rochelle's jaw sagged slightly. '*Gift* duty? I—I don't know.'

'When he does it might make him think again. The Government has a large mouth that is ever open,' Rex warned.

She sent a look of appeal to Justin then went on with a hint of defiance, 'Justin had *promised* me the formula for his special orange mix, so of course I wanted to buy the right bags of *whatever* to enable me to mix it.'

She paused again to look at Justin, but he made no comment apart from an abrupt, 'Do go on.'

'You can see how it was,' Rochelle said plaintively. 'I *needed* the formula—and it was too late in the evening to be disturbing Justin—so I took a torch and went to the shed, where I felt sure he kept his records. I shouldn't have gone there without his permission——'

'Or helped yourself to a sample to be analysed,' Justin put in.

'I *know*—and for that I'm *very*, *very* sorry.' She hung her head like a small child in disgrace, then peeped at him through hair that had fallen across one eye. 'Do you forgive me?'

'Yes, of course. Forget it.' Justin's tone and expression betrayed his irritation.

'Thank you.' Rochelle sent a beam round the table. 'Now I can enjoy this lovely lunch.'

But Rex had not finished with the subject. Fixing Rochelle with a stern eye, he said, 'I'm curious to know if you were able to procure the necessary commodities to make up this famous mix.'

She shook her head dolefully. 'No, I'm afraid not. Justin found me in the shed before I could write down all the details. He was out in the moonlight with your *typist*,' she added in an aggrieved tone.

The shaggy grey brows shot up. 'He was? Out in the moonlight, you say? Well, now—that's most interesting.' He turned and sent a direct stare towards Mary.

She felt her face go scarlet. 'We were only walking,' she said defensively. 'Nor would I have gone without Justin because I'm stupidly nervous in the dark.'

Laura spoke kindly to Mary. 'Don't be embarrassed, dear. Moonlight and roses have always been something to cherish.' She then turned to Ella with a change of subject. 'Tomorrow we must go to the supermarket in Gisborne. I've made quite a long list——'

Rochelle cut in eagerly, 'Mother *loves* the supermarket. She says it's a place where she meets people she hasn't seen for ages—or even *years*.' A small giggle escaped her.

Rex's tone was mildly curious as he queried, 'Is there something funny about meeting old friends?'

Rochelle nodded eagerly. 'Sometimes there is—it depends upon who the old friend happens to be.' A suppressed excitement seemed to grip her as she asked, 'Would it bore you if I tell you a story?' And, without waiting to learn whether or not it would, she went on. 'The last time I was at the supermarket with my parents it was Daddy who received a shock.' She fell silent, as though waiting for encouragement to go on.

'Why would that be?' Laura asked politely.

'Well, he came face to face with a person he hadn't seen for *years*, but he recognised her *instantly*. He just stood and gaped at her, then exclaimed, "Elizabeth!"' Rochelle paused to look at Rex coyly, her head on one side. 'Can you guess who she was, Mr Todd?'

He gave a snort of impatience, then demanded irritably, 'How the hell could I possibly do so? I'm not clairvoyant.'

Mary had caught her breath at the sound of her mother's name. Her heart had lurched, but had then settled down to a steady thump as she listened with apprehension. These people were about to lose confidence in her—she knew it instinctively—and she now cursed herself for her delay in explaining the situation. Justin, particularly, would censure her for not being entirely open, and the fact that it was Rochelle who was now bringing things to light positively infuriated her. Had Mother presumed she'd admitted her identity?

Rochelle sent smiles round the table. She knew she had their attention, but it was to Rex that she spoke.

'Daddy then explained that Elizabeth was your daughter. Now then—isn't that a surprise meeting?'

The old man's face had become a lined mask. 'I suppose it is—vaguely,' he admitted in a non-committal voice. 'So what about it?'

Rochelle's smile became even broader. 'Elizabeth then looked at me and asked if I'd met *her* daughter who was doing your typing.'

Justin spoke coldly, his voice gritting with anger. 'Is there more to this fascinating story, Rochelle? I suspect it's what you've really come to tell us—rather than to apologise to me. The apology was merely an excuse, and you came right on lunchtime to be sure of an audience.'

Laura was shocked by his words. '*Justin*, that was *very* rude. Rochelle is our *guest*.'

'It's the blasted truth,' he snapped.

Rochelle ignored most of what Justin had said by sending him a provocative grin. 'Yes, as it happens, there is more to this story. Later, as we drove home, Mother became quite cross with Daddy because he'd failed to introduce me to this person in the correct manner—and that she herself would've done it if only she'd been able to remember Elizabeth's *surname*. Daddy then explained that at the time he couldn't remember it either, but now that he'd given it more thought he recalled that she'd married a man named Alan Healey.'

There was silence in the room while all eyes focused on Mary. She longed to crawl under the table, but to do so would do nothing to remove the depression that was bearing down upon her. She also knew that something was expected of her, and that in truth she could find plenty to say, yet she did not speak.

And then Rochelle flung down her trump card. In a tone that could only be termed waspish she said, 'We're waiting to hear why Mary Healey is masquerading under the name of Mary Kendall.'

'This should be interesting,' Justin put in softly, his eyes narrowed as he watched Mary.

The words angered her, goading her to break her silence. Her eyes flashed blue sparks as she demanded furiously, 'Are you waiting for me to make a confession of some sort?'

His jaw tightened. 'I'm waiting to learn the right answers to several points that have puzzled me.'

'Like what?' she lashed at him.

'Like why you're here in the first place. You told me a vague story about wanting to look at a citrus orchard——'

'That is correct. What I did not add was that the orchard in question was my mother's old home. For years I'd heard so much about the Valencia, and here was my one and only opportunity to see it. Now do you understand?'

'Not quite,' he gritted. 'Why, for Pete's sake, didn't you come right in, knock at the door and tell us who you were?'

'Surely the answer to that lies in the extra pages of the memoirs,' she said pointedly, and, past caring whether or not she upset her grandfather, she added, 'I had no wish to be thrown out on my ear—while to *you* I'd be the daughter of the *deserter*, and quite beyond the pale.'

'I suppose you're right,' he admitted grudgingly.

'Now perhaps I can answer the question from the—er—principal speaker at this gathering.' She turned to Rochelle. 'You ask why I'm masquerading as Mary Kendall. The answer is simple. It's because I *am* Mary Kendall.'

'But Daddy said your mother married Alan Healey,' Rochelle said with determination.

'That's right—she did,' Mary confirmed. 'But *Daddy* didn't know that Alan died and that Mother married Peter Kendall, who came from Gisborne. I am the child of *that* marriage.' Sooner or later these details would have to be explained, she realised—therefore she might as well do it now.

'I don't believe you,' Rochelle snapped stubbornly.

Mary shrugged. 'My passport can prove my name and my age.'

'Then I want to see it. I want *proof*.' Rochelle's voice had risen to a higher pitch.

'You can go to hell,' Mary retorted. 'I don't have to prove anything to you. And that goes for anyone else who doubts my word,' she added, glaring across the table at Justin.

He retaliated by saying, 'But you did pose as a stranger to Rex, whereas in reality you were his granddaughter.'

'I *was* a stranger. I had never met him before.'

The old mán chuckled. 'Mary—I guessed who you were almost from the moment you arrived.'

Her eyes became round. 'You did?'

He nodded. 'When Justin brought you to us that first afternoon I thought Elizabeth was walking towards me. And then I realised you were too young to be Elizabeth, *but*, the moment you opened your mouth and began to talk, I heard Elizabeth's voice.'

She said, 'My father says that Mother and I sound exactly alike on the phone. He never knows which of us has answered.'

Rex said, 'Some voices are apt to implant themselves on the memory, and once there are never forgotten.'

'Why didn't you say something?' she asked while beginning to feel slightly foolish.

'Because I've been waiting for you to admit your identity to me.'

Laura spoke to Mary. 'What he says is true, dear. A few days after your arrival he confided to me that he felt sure you were Elizabeth's daughter.'

Mary turned to her grandfather again. 'Then you don't want me to leave at once? I'll quite understand if you do.'

He was shocked. '*Leave*? Before the memoirs are completely finished? Certainly not.'

Justin now leaned forward and spoke to Rochelle, his tone ironic. 'Tell me, dear neighbour—what did you hope to gain by these revelations?'

The blonde girl looked down at her empty plate as though searching for an answer, then, to give herself more time, she drank the last of her coffee.

As the silence continued Rex gave a throaty chuckle. 'Isn't it obvious she hoped I'd throw Mary out on her ear? Instead she's done us all a favour by bringing things out into the open and clearing the air.'

Laura agreed with him. 'Yes—of course—she has done just that. Thank you, Rochelle,' she added with a smile.

But Laura's words were not appreciated by Rochelle, who stood up and said petulantly, 'If you'll excuse me— I think it's time I went home. Mother will be wondering where I am.'

'She didn't suggest you come to drop your little bombshell?' Justin drawled silkily. 'No—I'm sure you were able to think up that one all by yourself. I'll see you to your car.' He pushed his chair from the table and followed her out of the room.

Mary thought for a moment then said hesitantly, 'I hate quarrels, and I don't like seeing her leave in such an unhappy frame of mind. Do you think it would help if I offered a hand of friendship?'

'You could try,' Laura said gently. 'But don't expect too much.'

Mary left the table to follow Justin and Rochelle, who were making their way towards a small yellow Mini which was parked near the packing shed. The sound of her steps on the gravel caused Rochelle to glance over her shoulder, and Mary was dismayed to see the blonde's face become contorted with anger.

'You're unable to leave us alone for five minutes?' the latter demanded aggressively.

'I—I thought that perhaps we could make friends——' Mary began in a timid voice.

Rochelle sneered. 'You've got to be joking.' Then she turned upon Justin angrily. 'You're a blind idiot if you can't see her little game.'

Mary felt bewildered. '*Game*? What are you talking about?'

Rochelle ignored her as she continued to address her remarks to Justin. 'That story about wanting to see her mother's old home is just a load of rubbish. She had far more than that in mind.' Her voice had risen to a higher pitch.

Justin regarded her with barely concealed impatience. 'Pray enlighten me—if you can control your temper.'

'I can control it all right,' she flashed at him. 'And I can see the situation very clearly. Her desire to see Mummy's old home was merely the excuse to get her here. Her plan was to meet the old man—her *grandfather*, you understand—and with luck she hoped to wheedle her way into his affections—the ultimate goal being a share in his estate.'

'That's not true,' Mary cried indignantly. 'Such a plan never entered my mind.'

'*Shut up*,' Rochelle hissed at her. 'The entire picture is as plain as day.' She turned to Justin again. 'Now you listen to me—if Mary and her mother are included in old Rex's estate it will affect the share that will go to your aunt. *Got it*?'

'Yes, I've got it. So what?' he snapped impatiently.

Rochelle became agitated. 'Are you so dim-witted you can't see that that's the entire reason for her being here?'

Mary gave a cry as she appealed to Justin. 'Please don't listen to her. What she says isn't true. Or is that what you really believe of me?' She looked at him anxiously, waiting for his reply, but he ignored her question.

Instead he spoke to Rochelle, his voice clipped with irritation. 'Laura's situation is not your business, Rochelle, so why you're uptight about it is something I'm unable to understand. However, as you appear to be making it your business, let me assure you that, apart from being entitled to a third of Rex's estate, she is very financially comfortable in her own right. On top of that she has an expense-free home with me for the rest of her life.'

Rochelle got into her Mini and slammed the door. She wound down the window and glared at Justin. 'OK—so Laura won't starve—but that's not the main issue.'

His mouth twisted with derision. 'The point you're overlooking, Rochelle, is that Laura is the last person in the world to object to Rex's including his daughter, or his granddaughter, in his estate. It's his money to leave as he chooses, so why don't you get yourself home and forget about things that don't concern you?'

'I *hate* you, Justin King,' she blazed at him. 'I'll never speak to you again.'

'Good. Make sure you keep to that promise,' he snapped.

The gear of the Mini was shoved into place with a grating sound and the small car shot down the drive with a spraying of tiny stones.

Mary sent an anxious glance towards Justin. She was acutely conscious of the fact that he had failed to answer the question she had put to him, and she wondered if the omission had been deliberate. To put it to the test she said hesitantly, 'Justin—you didn't tell me what I want to know.'

He regarded her bleakly, his jaw set. 'What *you* want to know? That's mighty rich. Doesn't it occur to you that there could be a small matter that I want sorted out?'

She shook her head vaguely. 'What do you mean? Please explain.'

But before he could do so one of the packers called to him from the shed door. 'Excuse me, boss—we're almost out of fruit in the shed. Has the orchard been stripped?'

Justin turned to answer him. 'No, there's plenty on the trailer. We took rather long over lunch, otherwise Rex would've had the tractor in the yard. I'll see to it.' He strode away without giving Mary a second glance.

Mary's lip trembled as she watched his departure. There's my answer, she thought bitterly. He *does* believe I came here with Grandfather's estate in mind. Rochelle has sown the seed, and it has taken root. Tears of anger filled her eyes as she walked back to the house.

Nor did she feel like returning to the dining-room to face the others, who, after talking among themselves, might also have decided she'd come to pave the way for a share in the estate. She then felt more than thankful that she'd kept quiet about her relationship with Rex Todd, and now the urge to finish the memoirs and leave the Valencia sent her hastening back to the office.

But here she was troubled by lack of concentration, with Justin's face coming between herself and the work. And although she kept hoping he would come in through the door that led outside there was no sign of him. Her depression deepened, and it was the arrival of Rex Todd that forced her to pull herself together.

He sat down heavily in the chair beside Justin's desk, then looked at her searchingly before he spoke. 'Well, young lady—there's just one thing I want to know.'

'Yes—Grandfather?' she queried in a meek voice. It was the first time she had applied the name to him, and she waited to see how he would take it.

He grinned. 'I've wondered when you'd come out with it. And I've also wondered if you intended leaving here without saying a word about who you are.'

'No—I planned to tell you just as I was leaving,' she admitted.

'Well, I'm glad you actually did intend to tell me— eventually.' He paused thoughtfully, his blue eyes glinting at her. 'What about your mother? Does she intend leaving New Zealand without coming to visit her old father?'

Mary felt she had to be frank about this question. 'Yes, I'm afraid so, Grandfather. I tried to persuade her, but she declared that wild horses wouldn't drag her near the place.'

He scowled. 'She did, did she? She was always very determined.'

Justin's voice spoke from the passage doorway. 'She sounds like a real chip off the old block.' His dark grey eyes rested upon Mary, holding her gaze as he said in a cynical tone, 'I presume you take after your mother?'

She kept her voice cool. 'I'm told I look like her, but in character I'm more like my father.' She felt frustrated. Justin, she suspected, had come to talk to her, but because her grandfather was there he was certain to go away again.

However, in this supposition she proved to be wrong because Rex opened the box of photographs, and Justin's interest was caught at once. He remained in the room while they were being sorted, and although he laughingly teased Rex about some of them, his attitude towards Mary was polite, yet aloof.

Eventually the photos had been gone through and placed in two piles comprising possibles and rejects. Rex then turned to Mary and said, 'It's time I got back to the tractor. I'll leave you to make the final choice of what goes in.'

Justin's brows rose. 'They're your memoirs,' he pointed out to Rex. 'Shouldn't you be the one to decide which photos go in?'

The old man grinned, then said with a hint of satisfaction, 'I'll leave it to my granddaughter. She'll know which ones are suitable to fit in with the script.'

Mary longed to shout with joy. 'My granddaughter', he'd said. It meant she'd been accepted as such, and while she ached to throw her arms about his neck she felt it would be unwise to do so in front of Justin, who would be sure to take a cynical view of the action.

Remaining calm only with an effort, she sent Justin a smile that caused the dimple in her cheek to flash in and out as she said, 'Perhaps you'd like to help me choose them. They need to be black and white glossy prints.'

'An excellent idea!' Rex exclaimed as he left the room.

But Justin made no attempt to choose photos. He merely studied Mary's face with a thoughtful frown on his handsome features while he drawled, 'So—he's "Grandfather" at last. You must be feeling very pleased with yourself.'

'Pleased?' She thought about it then said, 'Yes, I'm pleased that he now knows my identity. It gives me a much stronger feeling of having roots on my distaff side. It also gives me more time to learn about Mother's early family history than if I'd left it until the last minute before leaving.'

'Then you did intend to tell him—eventually?'

'Of course. It was just that your very *close friend*— the one with the *dowry*—brought things to a head.'

'She is *not* my very close friend,' he gritted angrily.

'She's a lot closer than you care to admit,' Mary snapped, now infuriated by the knowledge of this fact that was becoming so very definite in her mind.

'Where do you get this idea?' he rasped.

'It's simple. Only a *close* friend could brainwash you into believing I'd come here for a share in Rex Todd's estate.'

'What the hell makes you so sure I believe that?' he demanded through tight lips.

'Your attitude towards me—plus your disapproval, which has been written all over your face ever since lunchtime. As for the way your thoughts have been guided by her next door—well, that's more than obvious.'

He moved closer to stare down into her upturned face, an exclamation of extreme irritation escaping him. 'Now you listen to me! You are right on one count—but wrong on the other.'

'What do you mean?' His expression made her quail.

'You are right in assuming that I'm annoyed, although seething-mad would be a better word. It's coupled with bitter disappointment and the feeling of having been let down.'

His words left her feeling bewildered and dismayed. 'Justin, surely you're exaggerating. How could I possibly let you down?'

'By not being open and straightforward with me. From the moment I first held you in my arms I thought, Here is someone who is honest. It seems I was mistaken.'

Her chin rose. 'You're accusing me of being dishonest? I haven't told you a single lie about myself.'

'Nor the whole truth. It was deceitful to have kept your relationship to Rex a secret,' he declared in an accusing tone.

'Was it indeed?' Her head held high, she glared at him. 'Then hear this—my relationship to Rex was not your concern. Further, it was your own attitude which prevented me from telling you of it.'

'My attitude? What are you talking about?'

'Your antagonism towards women. Kittle cattle, you claimed. Have you forgotten your scathing comments regarding the daughter who deserted Rex? How could I possibly admit that I was *her* daughter?'

'Surely you could've trusted me to take a reasonable view of the situation. Hadn't my kisses told you anything?'

'Oh, yes—they told me plenty. They told me you needed to make love. But your words made it clear you intended to retain your own freedom at all costs.'

'Is it not possible for you to give me credit for changing those views?' he asked in a low voice.

She gave a short laugh. 'I'm afraid I'd take a lot of convincing.' Then a thought caused her to remind him of his earlier statement. 'You said I was right on one count, but wrong on the other. In what way was I wrong?'

'You were wrong in thinking I believed you had hopes of a share in Rex's estate. You're too independent to have such an idea.'

'Thank you for that much,' she said, sending him a bleak glance.

He left the room without further comment.

CHAPTER NINE

As THE door closed behind Justin, Mary's control left her. Her eyes filled with tears that rolled down her cheeks, and it was only when one splashed on a photo that she took a grip on herself. She dabbed at it with a clean handkerchief, hoping it would not be marked.

She then made decisions concerning the most suitable prints for reproduction, and was thankful to have gathered a few tips regarding the judging of them from her last employment. However, she knew her grandfather's assistance would be necessary for the captions.

He came in a short time later, apparently having thought of this point himself. 'You'll need help with what must go under the photos,' he said, his eyes regarding her searchingly.

She looked away from him. Had he noticed her pink eyelids? If so he made no comment, and for this she was grateful. 'The photos must all be numbered,' she informed him. 'And if we could make a list of the captions I'll type them in the morning—and that'll be the end of the job. You have read it all, I hope?'

'Yes—and I'm very satisfied. Thank you for being so patient with what I've been told is diabolical scrawl.'

They worked on the captions until it was time to go to the living-room, where they found Justin pouring drinks. Mary sent him a nervous glance while wondering if he was still cross with her, but he appeared to have regained his normal good humour, smiling affably as he handed her a sherry.

She remained cool, finding difficulty in wiping his accusations of dishonesty and deceit from her mind. A politely muttered 'Thank you' was her only response before moving to stand near the window, where her eyes rested on the closely shaven lawn with its trimmed edges. She knew that Justin had followed to stand behind her, and to break the silence that had fallen between them she said, 'It all looks so neat and tidy.'

'Yes. Ella's cousin from Wairoa has become settled in the bedroom off the back veranda. He's made a start on getting the garden under control. Ella's delighted to have him here—she's already added window-cleaning to his tasks.'

Mary chuckled. 'Ella will have him well organised.'

Justin moved closer to place a hand on her shoulder while pointing across the lawn. 'Those trees away to the right are the Valencias. That was the first variety of orange to be planted here.'

'Is that how the place got its name?' She looked at the trees, which had become golden-green in the rays of the setting sun. At the same time she tried to be nonchalant about the feel of his hand on her shoulder, yet it had the power to affect her. Nor did his hand make any move to draw her closer to him, despite the fact that Rex and Laura were no longer in the room, and the knowledge caused a sigh to escape her.

It did not escape his notice. 'What was that for?' he demanded.

'What was what for?' she hedged, moving away from him.

'I didn't imagine that deep sigh. Something is troubling you?'

'There's still so much I don't know about the place—and now it's too late.' A sad note had crept into her voice.

His brows shot up. 'Too late? Why would that be?'

'Because I've only one task to complete, and that's the typing of the illustration captions. Then it will be time for me to leave.'

He ignored her last words. 'Are you saying you haven't gathered an entire picture of the place from the memoirs?'

She frowned. 'I suspect that numerous details have been left out—the reason for calling it the Valencia being one small example. I'll see if I can include that snippet of information.'

Justin made excuses for Rex. 'He's an old man. His memory isn't what it once was.'

She sent him a rapid glance. 'Am I right in thinking you're rather fond of him?'

'Perfectly right. He's done all he can to help me with my orchard project. He's taught me all he knows.'

Across the lawn she watched the Valencias turning to a deeper green as the sun sank beyond distant hills. Her voice trembled slightly as she said, 'Tomorrow I should be finished by lunchtime or early afternoon. Would it be convenient for you to drive me back to Wainui?'

'That sounds as if you're anxious to leave as soon as possible,' Justin said, his voice betraying irritation.

Mary turned to him, her expression deadly serious. 'Not at all—but I'm sure it would be a tremendous relief to *you* to have your house cleansed of deceit and dishonesty.' The last words rang with bitterness.

Before he could make a reply Ella entered the living-room. 'Don't you two people want to eat this evening?' she asked. 'Laura is waiting to serve dinner—and there's somebody else becoming mighty impatient.'

'OK, we're coming,' Justin said to Ella, then to Mary he muttered, 'We'll continue with this discussion later.'

His words filled her with apprehension, and in an effort to brush them away Mary hurried to Laura's side. 'I'm sorry we've been holding up the meal,' she apologised. 'Can I help you serve? I'm sure you're missing Ella's assistance.'

Laura's smile was full of understanding. 'Bless her—she likes to have her meal in the kitchen with her cousin. It gives them the opportunity to talk over old family days. Ella says they lived near each other when they were young. Memories, you know.'

Rex's eyes held a far-away expression. 'Ah, yes—memories,' he murmured. 'Some are good, some are bad.'

Justin said, 'We all have to deal with memories, Rex. Recently I've trampled several underground.' He glanced at Mary.

She contemplated him thoughtfully. Was he telling her that the memory of his former love was no longer with him? Had he trampled underground all recollections of the woman who had let him down in preference for another man? To let him know she understood she said, 'I'm glad you've dealt with that hurt of distant days.'

He grinned in silent affirmation, then changed the subject by turning to Rex with a question. 'I've been wondering—apart from the satisfaction of actually recording these memoirs—for whom have you written them? They really have been a major task.'

Rex was silent for several long moments before he said, 'If you're really keen to know—I've recorded the history of the property, plus the history of the district's citrus-growing, for your own future grandchildren.'

Justin stared at him in a stunned manner until he said, 'Did you say for *my grandchildren*?'

Mary was unable to control the giggle that escaped her as she spoke to her grandfather. 'I'm afraid there won't be too many of those little toddlers around. Justin intends to remain fancy-free of all kittle cattle. He himself told me so—and I can assure you he was quite adamant about it.'

Justin was not amused. 'What gives only women the prerogative to change their minds?' he demanded testily.

Mary was unable to hide her surprise. Her laughter ceased as she asked, 'You're saying you've changed your mind about remaining fancy-free?'

'That's right,' Justin declared loftily. 'I've decided that the mind is made to be changed—otherwise it becomes static.'

His words sobered Mary. So Justin *did* intend to marry sooner or later, but in the meantime—and despite his kisses—he was looking anywhere but in *her* direction. The hurt within her became more acute, and this was reflected by the shadows in her eyes as she turned to him. 'You didn't tell me if it would be convenient for you to take me home tomorrow afternoon,' she said.

He hesitated, then his eyes became hooded as he admitted, 'To be honest, tomorrow wouldn't be the most suitable time—I have an appointment next door.'

'You mean with Rochelle?' Mary asked, making an effort to keep her voice casual. She knew it was not her concern, but she had to ask. *Rochelle*—after her last words to him as she was leaving?

His words cut into her thoughts. 'My appointment happens to be with her father. We'll be discussing a business matter.' And, as his tone indicated that this was a private affair, nobody made further enquiries.

Mary hesitated, then took courage and turned to Rex. 'What about you, Grandfather? Would it be possible for you to drive me home?'

He frowned, then shook his head. 'Sorry, my dear— when Justin is off the property it's my job to keep an eye on the running of the place. You understand?'

She bit her lip. 'Yes, I understand.' In fact she understood very well. It was all too clear that he had no intention of going to Wainui Beach, where he was likely to come face to face with her mother. He was determined that Mother would come to him, she realised.

Laura spoke gently. 'Would it be too much of a hardship for you to spend another night with us?'

'No, of course not,' Mary assured her hastily.

Laura went on, 'During the time you've been here we've seen so little of you. You've been locked in that office—in fact you've been little less than a slave to those memoirs.'

Mary turned to her grandfather. 'I hope they won't prove to be too costly. In Australia private publication such as this is anything but cheap, especially if only a few copies are run off.'

'I doubt that it'll put me into debt,' he remarked drily.

Later that evening when Rex and Laura had retired to bed, Mary again found herself standing beside Justin at the living-room window. Moonlight flooded the garden, illuminating it sufficiently to see the vigorous movement of nearby shrubs and trees.

Justin watched a thrashing branch then said morosely, 'They're here—the October gales. We get them every year. I'm afraid it's far too rough for a moonlight saunter among the trees.'

Mary caught her breath. 'Did you have such a thought in mind?' she queried, her voice betraying surprise.

He hesitated before admitting, 'I thought it would be pleasant—considering you're so determined to make this your last evening at the Valencia.'

'Didn't you hear me promise to stay another day? Perhaps tomorrow evening?' She looked at him hopefully.

He shook his head. 'It's a southerly, which is usually something that lasts for two or three days. Despite our shelter the ground will be covered with fallen fruit. I'll invite children from the nearest school to come and help themselves.'

'You're very generous——' she began.

'Nonsense. I'm merely using the easy way of getting the windfalls up off the ground. And if it gives the children a treat—well, that'd be satisfactory. However, I'll wait till the wind drops before I phone the headmaster to pass on the message.'

He's thoughtful towards everyone except myself, she mused while staring through the glass. He really doesn't want to walk in the orchard with me. Secretly he's pleased there's a horrible wind blowing its head off out there— even if it does bring the fruit down. It lets him off nicely. A cloud of depression wrapped itself about her, and as she turned from the window to sit on the settee her dejection became more visible than she realised.

Justin regarded her critically. 'Finishing the memoirs doesn't appear to have put you in the mood to jump over the moon. Quite the reverse, in fact. Am I right in suspecting that something bothers you?'

She made no reply, being unable to deny the truth of his words.

He came to sit beside her on the settee. 'Why not share the trouble and therefore halve it?' he suggested.

She looked at him bleakly. Share the trouble? Admit that she loved him, but that her love was unreturned? No way would she utter such a statement. Nor would she admit how deeply his hurtful accusations of deceit and dishonesty had cut into her soul.

'Well, come on—out with it,' he urged gently, then his voice suddenly took on a harsher note. 'Or are there more facts you're determined to keep hidden from me? If so I'll question you no further.'

She shook her head. 'No—no—it's nothing like that——'

'Then it's something that has happened round here?' he pursued.

'Yes—I suppose so.' Her misery grew while she raked her brains for a reason that would cause her to feel low-spirited, and then one that was genuine leapt into her mind. It enabled her to say, 'It's Mother and Grandfather. I've been hoping to see a way of bringing them together. After all, she's his only child, but she's as stubborn as he is. Neither will go to the other, and the moment we leave Gisborne it will be too late.' She looked down at her hands. And too late for us, she thought, her expression becoming pathetic.

Justin said, 'I can understand how you feel, but I'm unable to see what you can do about it. They are adults and must solve this matter between themselves.'

'Adults!' she exclaimed angrily. 'They're behaving like sulky children. Grandfather should be setting an example to his daughter, while Mother should be setting an example to me.'

Justin laughed as the situation began to strike him as being humorous. 'A pair of stubborn fools,' he chortled.

But Mary did not find the situation to be funny. 'It's not a laughing matter,' she declared indignantly. 'Life is too short for a quarrel of such length.'

'Life is too short for any sort of quarrel,' he responded on a more sober note. 'But even if you did manage to bring them face to face they'd probably only snarl at each other.'

'How can you be so sure of that?'

'Because I suspect that each lacks confidence in the other's reaction.' He turned and faced her on the settee, then added accusingly, 'Just as you had so little faith in my understanding of the situation that you were unable to admit your connection to Rex.'

'Huh—hark at who's talking,' she flared. '*You* were suspicious of *me* from the first moment of meeting. You were positive I was here with an ulterior motive. What sort of faith in my integrity is *that*, may I ask?'

He stared at her, frowning, then moved a few inches closer while his eyes scanned every inch of her face. 'At that time I was the proverbial doubting Thomas.'

Mary knew it was only an excuse for his distrust, but she held his gaze steadily, her heart beating a little faster while she waited for him to move even closer. Did he intend to kiss her? She swallowed nervously, then decided to play it cool, and although she longed to tilt her face upward she kept her chin at its present level. 'You're no longer quite as doubting?' she asked.

'No. I'm seeing the situation much more clearly—all too clearly in fact.' His jaw hardened.

She felt puzzled. 'The situation?'

'The situation between us. Or hadn't you recognised the remote possibility of a situation between us?' He drew back, then stood up to cross the room and turned on the television.

It was then Mary knew she'd made a mistake. Instead of showing a little warmth she'd been too cool—too casual. She hadn't taken his offered hand or even met him halfway. She was a dumb fool, she told herself.

Justin watched the screen for several moments before he said, 'I don't know what's on, but it might interest you. Personally, I'm going to bed with a book, so if you'll excuse me I'll say goodnight.'

After he'd left the room she continued to crouch on the settee while berating herself with a few home-truths. 'You, my girl, are growing more like your mother every day,' she muttered. 'This is the sort of attitude she's held towards Grandfather—too proud to make the first move. Now then—if you possess one ounce of brain you'll tap on Justin's door and kiss him goodnight.'

She stood up, full of determination to do just that— but when she reached the door leading into the passage another thought struck her. Had he indicated that he had any *real* feelings for her? No—it was merely wishful thinking on her part; therefore she watched another programme, then switched off the TV and went to bed.

But although the bed was warm and comfortable sleep evaded her, and as she lay wide-eyed in the darkness she thought of life without the nearness of Justin. It would begin tomorrow evening after he'd driven her home, and after that she would no longer be able to watch the changing expressions on his handsome face, or hear the sound of his deep voice.

It will be like suffering a bereavement, she thought, then realised that when people lost a loved one life had to go on just the same. But for herself it would be a long time—if ever—before another man replaced Justin in her heart. After that the tears began to fall, rolling down to soak into the pillow.

Next morning she slept later than usual. She felt unrefreshed and heavy-eyed, and when she went into the kitchen for breakfast she was surprised to find Justin still there. She then became conscious of his critical scrutiny of her face.

'You've had a sleepless night,' he accused while standing up to pull out her chair. 'What kept you awake?'

'Where are the others?' she asked, ignoring his question.

'Rex is already out in the orchard—but Laura and Ella are in the storeroom making a list for the next visit to the supermarket. As for George, you'll find him in the vegetable garden. So as we have the room to ourselves you can pour your midnight troubles into my ear. I'm willing to listen,' he added while watching her face.

Mary remained silent. His was the last ear on earth into which she could pour her midnight troubles, but she knew he expected an answer. And then he solved the problem for her.

'Are you still worrying about how to bring your mother and old Rex together?' he asked.

'Yes—yes—that's it.' She grasped at the suggestion eagerly.

He eyed her narrowly. 'You're lying,' he accused softly. 'If that had been the reason you'd have said so at once. What a stubborn family you are—from the oldest to the youngest.'

She shook her head. 'I'm not as stubborn as Mother or Grandfather.'

'The exception being when it comes to confiding in me,' he pointed out in a dry tone. 'Then you can be *mighty* stubborn. Well, I can take the hint to mind my own damned business, except that I can't help wondering if it would be presumptuous of me to shove in an oar. That's if the opportunity arises, of course.'

'You mean, to bring them together?'

'Exactly.' His tone had become curt.

'I'd be most grateful—although I'm afraid time is running out. You'll be driving me home tomorrow, and after that the distance between us...' She paused, unable to go on as the thought of being so far from him brought a lump to her throat, and a slight tremble to her lower lip.

Justin gave no sign of having noticed these momentary indications of despondency. Instead he said, 'I'd better go. I must see to matters in the packing shed.'

Surprised, she said, 'You mean, you've waited to talk to me before going to the shed?'

'Of course. Why should it amaze you? I'll be seeing little of you today apart from lunchtime.' He went to the door then paused to look back. 'Incidentally, George told Ella he'd seen nothing of you. He's wondering if we keep you under lock and key. If the wind drops sufficiently for you to go for a walk, give him a kind word about his garden.'

She glanced through the window. 'It's still blowing a gale. I doubt that I'll be out walking today.'

But the noise of the wind failed to disturb her as she settled down to numbering the back of each photo, using a soft pencil to guard against damage. She then spent more time than she realised examining the photos, some of which included her mother and grandparents in their younger days. Their places in the manuscript were then indicated, and by that time it was midday with Laura coming to the door to tell her it was lunchtime.

Conversation at the table was general, although Justin appeared to have little to say. His handsome face remained serious, and his mind seemed to be occupied with thoughts he was unwilling to share.

Watching him, Mary was unable to resist voicing her concern. 'Are you worried about something, Justin?'

Her question surprised him. 'Worried? Not in the least. Why should I be worried?' He looked at her with interest.

'I thought that perhaps it was because the wind had brought so much fruit down. Is there a lot of fruit on the ground?' she asked.

He gave a slight shrug. 'I've no idea. I haven't troubled to look, but you can bet there'll be plenty.'

Rex spoke to Mary. 'He's been in a brown study throughout lunch. He's probably cooking up a new brew for his oranges. It'll be simmering in his mind. More blood and bone to the mixture, perhaps.'

Justin grinned. 'Well—as you're nearly dead from curiosity—how would the idea of enlarging the orchard grab you?'

They looked at him in stunned silence until Rex said, 'I don't see how you can do that unless—it's through Rochelle...'

But Justin refused to enlighten him. He merely looked smug as he said, 'All in good time—my plan will be revealed. Now if you'll excuse me I have things to do before keeping my appointment next door.' He stood up hastily and left the room.

Ella, who had entered in time to hear most of this conversation, watched Justin's departing back. 'Don't tell me he's off to collect the dowry,' she said querulously. 'I don't think I could stand it.'

Rex scowled, his jaw jutting ominously as he muttered, 'If he brings that wench here *I'll kill him.*'

Laura tried to soothe him. 'But Rex, dear—it's what you've wanted for so long.'

He thumped the table and roared, 'Damnation, woman, I've changed my mind—I couldn't care less now about that orchard.'

Mary felt she'd had enough. She sprang to her feet as she said, 'If you don't mind I'll go back to the office. I've still the captions to type.' Then she left the room, fortunately reaching the passage before it was necessary to dab at her eyes.

When she reached the office she almost flung herself into the chair, and to control her mind she concentrated upon the captions. Banging at the keys seemed to relieve her, and she had just completed the list when Rex entered the room.

Mary straightened her back and stretched her arms. 'There you are, Grandfather—it's all yours.'

He looked at the box of numbered photographs, then picked up the manuscript. Holding it almost reverently, he admitted, 'I'm glad you persuaded me to include those extra pages, which make it more complete.' Then, after hesitating for several moments, he asked casually, 'What happened to Alan Healey?'

Mary smiled inwardly. He's really asking about Mother via Alan Healey, she thought with a sense of satisfaction, then told him about the man's demise and of her mother's later life. Secretly, he's interested in learning about what happened to her, she decided.

Eventually Rex said, 'I'm glad things turned out well for her.' He took a wallet from an inner pocket of his jacket and added, 'Now then—I'll write a cheque for you.'

'Which I shall not accept,' she said quietly and with determination.

His jaw jutted at her. 'I said, I shall write a cheque for you.'

'OK—you do that, Grandfather. Then you can watch me tear it to shreds. I don't think you realise that I've been more than paid by just being here—and by finding my roots through your memoirs. And in finding you and Laura.'

'And Justin?' he queried softly. 'Haven't you found more than you bargained for in that quarter?'

She looked down at her hands, then decided to be honest. 'Yes, I suppose I have—but Justin must follow his heart. If he has now discovered he loves Rochelle—well, that will be that.'

'Damned young idiot—I'll have his guts for garters.'

She moved to look at swaying branches through the glass of the door leading outside. 'It's still very windy,' she remarked, making an effort to get away from the subject of Justin.

'Yes. I've sent the pickers home. I thought it was too rough to be up ladders.'

She sighed. 'I suppose I'd better attend to packing my suitcase.'

He hesitated then said with an almost pleading note, 'Mary, promise you'll keep in touch. Promise you'll write to your old grandfather. I don't want to lose you completely.'

'Yes, of course—I promise.' She turned and hugged him, then hurried to her room, where she dragged her suitcase from beneath the bed. As she did so she knew that this was the moment she'd been dreading, and that soon she'd be leaving the Valencia forever.

It took little time to pack the few belongings she'd brought, and, after leaving the case open for last-minute items, she went to the kitchen, where the activity caused her to pause at the door. 'Is this a marmalade factory?' she asked, eyeing the bench and table laden with citrus fruit.

Laura paused in the act of weighing sugar. 'I'll admit it looks very much like it. We're making it to be sold to raise funds for the Red Cross Society. George is doing sterling work with the food processor, and Ella is searching for more jars. We're inclined to run short of them when we make so much.'

Mary took a deep breath. 'It smells wonderful. Can I help?'

'No, thank you, dear—there's nothing for you to do. It's a pity the wind is so strong, otherwise you could take a pleasant stroll in the orchard.' Laura tipped the sugar into the fruity mixture bubbling in the large pan on the stove.

Mary thought for a few moments. 'I'll go for a short walk,' she said, but did not add that the turmoil of the wind fitted the chaos in her own mind. Justin had assured her there would never be anything between himself and Rochelle, yet there he was, next door making arrangements—for what?

She recalled the afternoon when he had taken her to see the pickers at work, and the evening of their walk in the moonlight, and suddenly she was gripped by an overwhelming desire to retrace the steps of those occasions. Even without Justin at her side, and despite the strong wind, it would be something to remember.

The coat she put on buttoned down the front, and she was thankful for its protection, especially as it was now late in the afternoon. Nor had she gone far before she realised that walking without Justin beside her was a recipe for depression. Nevertheless she pushed on, battling against the wind, and finding herself appalled by the sight of so much fruit lying on the ground.

As she approached the fertiliser shed the noise from its sheltering trees was like a muted roar, then, as she drew closer to the small building, she realised that the door was open. Justin, she recalled, had spoken of attaching a padlock to the door, but had probably failed to attend to this task. Even so, the wind should not have lifted the heavy bar that held the door closed.

She went forward with the intention of closing it, then stood still to stare incredulously at the person within. Rochelle, bending over the bench, was busily writing in a pad. Beside her, and lying open, was the book in which Justin kept details of his formulas for fertilising the various species of citrus fruits.

Mary stepped into the shed. 'You are a thief, Rochelle,' she declared scathingly. 'This is the second time you've tried to steal Justin's orange formula.'

Rochelle swung round to confront Mary, her face turning first white and then crimson. She looked through the door to make sure Justin was not there, then launched into the attack. 'Don't you dare call me a thief,' she spat. 'Justin promised me the formula and I intend to have it.'

'But he hasn't given it to you—therefore you are stealing it,' Mary pointed out. 'I suppose you could see that the wind had caused the pickers to leave and that you could come here unseen.'

'I didn't have to do that,' Rochelle declared loftily. 'Justin told me to come here and help myself.'

'Where and when did this happen?' Mary asked doubtfully. Was it possible that Justin had reconsidered? she wondered. Yes—of course it was possible if what she feared was about to come to pass. 'Well, *where* and *when*?' she persisted.

Rochelle became evasive. 'Oh—near the tangelos—a short time ago. Anyhow, it has nothing to do with you.'

A laugh escaped Mary. 'I think you're lying,' she said, the doubts clearing as her love for Justin refused to allow her to believe he'd marry Rochelle.

'You're entirely wrong,' Rochelle snapped, tossing her head in a haughty manner. 'Why don't you go back to that *stupid* typewriter and get that *stupid* job finished?'

'I finished it this afternoon,' Mary informed her calmly.

'Oh. So now I suppose you're out searching for Justin,' Rochelle sneered.

'Not really. I know exactly where Justin happens to be.' Mary went closer to the bench to see how much Rochelle had written on the pad. Obviously, she'd been busy for some time.

'OK—so where is he?' Rochelle demanded aggressively.

'At your house. He had an appointment with your father this afternoon. I thought you'd have known that.'

'No, I didn't know.' Rochelle was clearly bewildered. 'I'd better go home and see what it's about.' She paused to look at Mary suspiciously. 'You are telling me the truth, I hope?'

Mary shrugged. 'Why should I bother to lie about it?'

Rochelle lifted her pad from the bench. 'It seems strange. I mean, when Justin comes to our house it's to see me—not my father.' She pushed Justin's book closer to Mary. 'There—see if you can decipher those formulas.' Then she turned to leave.

Mary bent over the book. It was the first time she had seen Justin's handwriting, and she was interested to see the neat but firm formation of the letters. But even as she looked at the words that meant little to her the shed was suddenly darkened as the closing door shut out the daylight.

Rochelle's ringing laugh, coupled with the sound of the door bar being shot into place, told Mary she was now locked in the shed. She screamed and hammered at the door, but there was no response.

CHAPTER TEN

THE sound of the bar being pushed into place had sent a shock of fear through Mary's system. Her frenzied efforts to wrench it open were of no avail, and as she struggled she heard Rochelle's high-pitched laughter on the other side of the door.

Knowing the blonde girl was there, Mary shouted to her. 'Rochelle—*Rochelle*—please open the door. *Rochelle—let me out——*'

Rochelle's voice came mockingly above the sound of the wind. 'Try and get yourself out. I'm going home.'

Mary became desperate. 'You know I can't open the door—there's no latch on this side—*please let me out*.'

'You can wait there till somebody finds you—and I hope it takes a long time.' Another laugh rose on the air, echoing faintly above the noise in the high branches of sheltering trees.

'Rochelle—*Rochelle*—please—*please* let me out—*open the door, please——*'

There was no reply, and after a period of anxious listening to hear the bar being removed Mary's pleadings turned to panic. Her screams filled the shed as she hammered at the inside of the door until eventually she was forced to realise that Rochelle was no longer there. She had gone home, leaving her to be found at a later date—how much later being anyone's guess.

The thought reminded her that the household would begin to worry. Grandfather and George would be out searching for her and no doubt Justin would join in when he arrived home. But, with the bar across the outside of the door, would any of them consider looking inside the shed? No—of course not. She couldn't possibly be in there, they'd decide. Nor was the shed a place where

171

anyone went to frequently. Fertilising was a seasonal task, and she could be dead before she was found.

In the meantime the thought of being there all night, quite apart from the fear of not being found for several days, was sufficient to cause a renewed surge of hysterical panic-filled screaming and hammering at the door until at last she sank to the floor in a state of exhaustion. Spasms of uncontrolled sobbing then shook her until draughts of cold air sweeping in under the door made her scramble to her feet.

By that time the fading daylight, coming only from the small high window, had caused objects in the shed to become almost invisible. Mary knew that soon the place would be pitch-dark, and in the deepening gloom she went to the bench, where she closed the formula book and pushed weighing equipment aside.

She then clambered up on to the bench in an effort to reach the window, but while she was able to push it open a fraction it was too small for her to climb through. Nevertheless she spent time shouting for help, hoping desperately that someone would hear, but her calls were flung back in her face by the wind. Suddenly her voice gave out, and she could do little better than utter noises that were no more than pathetic croaks.

Frustrated, and shaking with fury that Rochelle should put her through this ordeal, Mary climbed down and leaned despondently against the bench. And then the sound of a scuffle caught her ear. Had Rochelle returned to set her free? Her eyes strained towards the door, waiting for it to open, but nothing happened. It must have been her imagination, she decided.

But no—the scuffling came again, this time closer and accompanied by the grinding of teeth. Terrified, her heart leapt as she recognised the presence of a rat, and in an instant she was back on the bench, where she crouched against the wall while staring through the darkness at the floor.

And then the pungent odours of the various fertilisers rose about her, filling her lungs until she felt nauseated.

Previously, she had told herself she'd become accustomed to them, but now they were forcing themselves upon her until she began to feel ill.

The feeling of sickness caused her to stand at the window once more, and she lifted her face to breathe in great gulps of air until the dizziness left her. Then she settled back on the bench, sobbing while she listened to the wind.

Nor was it long before her old fears of the dark began to grip her with icy fingers. They brought on a fresh attack of trembling until, despite the discomfort of a cramped position on the hard wooden bench, exhaustion caused her to fall into a restless sleep.

Mary had no idea how long she had slept before she was awakened by a light shining on her face and the sound of Justin's voice in her ears.

'What the hell are you doing in here?' he demanded, his voice echoing amazement.

Hoarsely, she could utter only one word. 'Rochelle——'

He stared at her incredulously. '*Rochelle*? Are you saying she shut you in here?'

She nodded wordlessly while tears of relief rolled down her cheeks.

'The *bitch*.' Then his arms went about her, holding her against him. 'My poor darling—they said you went for a walk hours ago. We've been off our heads with anxiety, we've tramped over every inch of the orchard, fearing you were lying injured, perhaps hit by a falling branch or tree.'

She scarcely heard his words. Had he called her *darling*? She lifted her face to look at him wonderingly, then found it being covered with kisses while he murmured endearments in a husky voice that was anything but steady.

'Were you really worried about me?' she asked in a small voice.

'Darling,' he murmured again. 'Darling Mary—I've been almost out of my mind.'

The words filled her with such satisfaction that she was unable to speak, and instead she could only look at the light in his eyes as they were caught by the beam of his torch.

'Don't you know that I love you?' he asked soberly.

'How could I know unless you'd told me? You gave me the impression you were disgusted with me,' she quavered.

'I was flaming mad because you hadn't confided in me. I was sure my love for you must have been more than obvious, yet you were unable to trust me sufficiently to admit who you were. Are you saying it has come as a surprise?'

'A shock is more like it—although actually there were times when I thought—and hoped——' Tears filled her eyes.

His arms tightened about her. 'You hoped?'

'Oh, yes—I hoped you'd say you loved me enough to break your determination to remain fancy-free.'

'Was that to pander to your feminine vanity?'

'No—foolish man—it was because I love you——'

Her words were cut off as his lips found hers and they clung together until at last he said, 'For Pete's sake let's get out of here.' Then he lifted her from the bench as though she were a small child and carried her outside.

It was wonderful to be out of the shed; it was glorious to feel his arms about her. It was like a dream to know that he loved her, and even as she revelled in the knowledge Mary looked about her and realised that all was silent. 'Justin—the wind has dropped.'

He pushed the bar in place then took her in his arms again. Looking down into her face, he said, 'Yes, that particular storm has passed, but no doubt there will be others. Are you willing to weather them with me? I'm asking you to marry me.'

She reached up to entwine her arms about his neck. 'I wish I had a better voice with which to say yes—yes—yes,' she croaked.

'I shouldn't be allowing you to speak at all just now, but there are a few things I'm anxious to learn—like how you came to be shut in the shed.'

At that moment a light came towards them. Justin flashed his torch to indicate their position, and as the man reached them Mary gazed up at a large policeman. The latter looked at Mary, then spoke to Justin. 'Is this the young lady, Mr King?'

'Yes. I'm afraid she's been locked in this shed for several hours,' Justin explained, then introduced them. 'Constable Perry—Miss Kendall.'

The constable examined the bar across the door. 'Not much hope of moving that from the inside,' he remarked. 'How did it happen, miss? Who locked you in?'

Mary remained silent, her only desire being to forget the entire episode, especially at this particular moment when she was longing to be back in Justin's arms. 'I—I'd rather not say,' she whispered at last.

But Justin did not agree with her reticence. 'The constable must be told, Mary,' he said in a firm voice. 'He's come all the way from Gisborne to organise a search.' He then turned to the constable with further explanation. 'She was locked in the shed by our neighbour's daughter. It could've been days before she was found.'

'You'll be pressing charges, no doubt?' Constable Perry queried.

Mary spoke huskily. 'No—no—I'd prefer to forget about it.'

'We'll consider the question, Constable,' Justin declared with determination. 'Rochelle must learn she can't lock people in sheds until they lose their voices through screaming for help.'

'You're quite right,' Perry agreed. 'She should be taught a lesson. Well, I'll be on my way. I'll inform the household that the young lady has been found and that there's no further need to wander round in the dark.' He sent Justin a sharp glance. 'You will be in soon, I presume?'

'As soon as I've cleared a few details in my mind,' Justin assured him.

'Good. The young lady will be in need of food, you understand.'

As soon as the constable had left them Justin took Mary in his arms again. 'Now then, my darling—I'm curious to know what took you to the shed?'

Shyly, she told him, 'I wanted to walk where we had walked, and that brought me here, where I found Rochelle taking notes for the second time. We argued, and it was only when I told her that you had gone to visit her father that she decided to rush home.'

'Shutting the door firmly behind her,' Justin said grimly, his arms tightening about Mary. 'By that time her father and I would have been in Gisborne.'

'*Gisborne*?' she echoed. She was revelling in the feel of his jacket against her cheek, but his last words forced her to draw back and stare up into his face. 'Why would you both go to Gisborne?'

He kissed her upturned brow then asked teasingly, 'Shall I tell you now—or are you so near starvation you'd prefer to go back to the house for food?'

'No, no—tell me *now*,' she pleaded, alive with curiosity.

'It's rather a long story,' Justin prevaricated. 'I should really take you back to the house for some of Ella's excellent broth.'

'I'm not hungry. I can last for ages——'

'You know they'll be waiting for us to come in.'

'You're a *wretch*, Justin King. Tell me *at once*—or the marriage is off,' she warned with what seriousness she could muster.

He sighed. 'Well, that's something I dare not risk. As it happens, Grover and I were visiting my solicitor.'

'Your solicitor? I don't understand.'

'OK—I'll start at the beginning. When I was told that Susan and Bob Grover had ideas of retiring to the Queensland Gold Coast I was not surprised because I know they love that area. But the story of the orchard being put into Rochelle's name didn't ring true to me. It had the strong smell of a carrot being dangled before my nose.'

Mary reached up to kiss his chin. 'Dearest donkey—don't you know that carrots are good for you? They help you to see better in the dark. The carotene in them turns to vitamin A.'

'I believe you because this carrot showed me the way,' Justin continued. 'I went to Bob Grover and told him I'd heard he was breaking his neck to get to the Gold Coast. He admitted this to be a fact, but that there was the matter of the orchard hanging over his head.'

'Did you tell him you'd heard that Rochelle was to take it over?'

'I did. He declared that that would be the day! He then told me that it was entirely his wife's idea, and that he, personally, lacked confidence in Rochelle's ability to run the place successfully.'

'So what happened then?' Mary asked, still wondering why a visit to a solicitor would be necessary.

'I offered to buy the orchard from him,' Justin admitted in a matter-of-fact tone and as though this were an everyday occurrence. 'We agreed on a price and he seemed unable to believe his luck. He was more than willing to accompany me to my solicitor there and then. Perhaps he feared I'd change my mind. However, the deed of sale has now been signed and the deposit paid.'

'Poor Rochelle,' Mary whispered, her hoarse voice full of compassion. 'She's lost you, and she's lost the orchard as well.'

'Don't let me hear you wasting sympathy on her,' Justin retorted crisply. 'You can only lose a possession, and she owned neither the orchard nor myself.'

'But she had hopes,' Mary said, still feeling sorry for Rochelle.

'We all have hopes, my darling. And, speaking of ownership, I take possession of the property at the end of next month.'

'That sounds—very soon.'

'That's because I want us to be married very soon. That house will be our new home. I'm hoping you'll like it. There are lovely views from the upstairs windows. I can assure you that Susan Grover has spent much money in making it exactly to her liking.'

'Because she hoped Rochelle would continue to live in it with you, I suppose.'

'Perhaps, although I doubt it. It's more likely that Susan did it for herself. Now then, enough of all this. If we don't return to the house there'll be another search party combing the orchard.' But before moving he took her in his arms again and kissed her deeply.

As they walked through the darkness towards the homestead Mary asked shyly, 'When shall we tell them about—us?'

'You can leave that task to me,' he promised. 'I'll choose the appropriate moment, but in the meantime you can prepare yourself for another surprise.'

'Another?' She looked at him wonderingly. 'There was the surprise of learning you love me—and the surprise of your orchard purchase. Do surprises always come in threes?'

'In this case they appear to have done so.' He led her through the secluded garden near the office, but instead of entering the house by its door he guided her further on towards the parking area in front of the packing shed.

Her eyes widened at the sight of a small car. 'That's Gran's Honda,' she croaked.

'That's right,' he commented drily.

'Does this mean that my parents are here?'

'Right again. The moment I heard you were missing I phoned your mother to ask if—for some reason—you'd hitch-hiked a ride home. She told me in no uncertain terms that you would *never* hitch-hike. I then explained that you seemed to have disappeared and that we were rather worried. I suggested she come to join the search.'

Mary began to giggle. 'Mother—whom wild horses wouldn't drag here—is actually here?'

'Wild horses haven't the power of a missing daughter. She said they'd come at once. They were here in such double-quick time, that little Honda must have sprouted wings.'

'How—how did Grandfather take her arrival?' Mary asked, wishing she'd been there to see it for herself.

'He didn't say a word. He merely held his arms open and she went into them like a homing pigeon.'

'What happened next?'

'Laura and Ella burst into tears. Rex blew his nose and your father suggested they got on with the search. A few minutes later the police car arrived, because, naturally, I hadn't wasted time in reporting the situation to them. It put an end to the weeping and blowing of noses.' He held her in a close embrace then asked, 'Are you ready to go in and face them now?'

'Not quite. There are two questions I'd like to ask. The first is, did you phone Rochelle to ask if I happened to be with her?'

'I did.' His voice shook with anger. 'She assured me she hadn't seen you all day.'

Mary felt a shrinking coldness within herself. 'I don't think anyone has ever hated me to such an extent,' she quavered.

Justin gripped her shoulders and shook her gently. 'Forget her—she's not worth a second thought.' His tone was little short of a command. 'What was your other query?'

'I've been wondering what caused you to look inside the shed.'

'Desperation, I think. George had already been searching in that area, but the bar across the door told him it was impossible for anybody to be inside the shed. However, the thought of the place nagged at me. I kept thinking of the walk we'd had in the moonlight, so I followed the route we'd taken, and of course it led me to the shed. I unbarred the door—and there you were.'

She gave a small shaky laugh. 'Darling—it was memory of our moonlight walk that took me to the shed.'

They clung to each other in silence while his lips trailed from her brow to her throat, then he put her from him firmly and led her back to the office door. But here the light shining through the glass made them pause, and, moving closer, they had a view of Rex Todd and his daughter. His arm was about her shoulders as, standing side by side, they stood gazing up at the portrait.

Justin put his lips to Mary's ears. 'We'll enter by the back door,' he whispered. 'They need their moments together.'

Mary nodded, her heart full of gratitude. Who else but Justin would be so thoughtful for her mother and grandfather?

Within the next few minutes she found herself to be the centre of attention, being greeted as one having returned from another world. There were cries of relief followed by hugs and kisses from all sides, while the ever-practical Ella simply led her to the kitchen table, where she placed a bowl of nourishing broth before her.

The small woman's words were firm. 'She'll not answer a single question until she finishes that lot and then some more.'

Later, as they sat drinking coffee in the living-room, Mary looked at each person in turn. These are my dearest people, she thought. In all the world they are the ones closest to me—yet this is the first time I've seen them together.

Justin and her father were deeply engrossed in holding a post mortem over a recent rugby match, while Laura and her mother appeared to have discovered complete compatibility. Ella, of whom she had grown fond, was serving her grandfather with more seed cake, at the same time warning him that it was his third large slice. George, Mary was told, had retired to bed, furious with himself for having failed to look in the shed.

She had already told them how she had come to be locked in the shed, and their wrath against Rochelle had echoed round the room.

'Of course you'll lay charges,' Rex had thundered. 'It's an assault that could have had serious consequences.'

But Mary had closed the discussion by saying that she really didn't feel like doing anything about it, and that it was better forgotten. Privately, she felt sorry for Rochelle, who had lost any hope of marriage to Justin. And when she learnt he'd purchased the orchard she'd hoped to take over, and that he'd be taking his bride to live in the house she called home, her rage would be beyond all measure.

Rex's voice cut into her thoughts as he spoke to her mother. 'We'll be sorry to see you take Mary back to Australia, Elizabeth,' he said gruffly. 'We've become very fond of her.'

Elizabeth glanced at her husband. 'Well, actually, we've got news for Mary. Whether or not she'll be pleased about it is another matter, and remains to be seen.'

Peter Kendall said, 'We might as well tell her about it now.'

His words caused Mary to sit up and take notice. 'What are you talking about?' she exclaimed.

Elizabeth sent Peter another rapid glance then said, 'I'm talking about our returning to live in New Zealand. I hope you won't mind too much, dear.'

'Mind? Why should I mind?' Mary asked casually while hiding her inner delight.

Elizabeth went on, 'Of course it will be an upheaval, but your father has taken a liking to the leisurely life in his old home town.'

'Everything is so much easier,' Peter explained. 'I can park my car without any trouble, I don't have to pay the earth to belong to the local golf club—nor drive too many miles to reach it. I already have a house here, nicely situated beside the sea, and I feel as if I've come home. Your mother is in full agreement with the idea, therefore we've withdrawn the house from sale. So what do you think, Mary?'

Before Mary could say anything Justin answered for her. 'I can assure you she thinks it's a marvellous idea, because now is the time to admit she has no intention of returning to Sydney. She will be remaining here—as my wife.'

The announcement brought a stunned silence until everyone began talking at once with cries of gladness, felicitations and congratulations filling the air.

Rex said, 'My boy—I thought you'd never come to your senses.'

A quick glance of amusement passed between Laura and Ella, who tactfully refrained from reminding Rex of his previous ambitions for Justin and the neighbouring orchard.

And then Laura began looking ahead as she said, 'Changes will be made in this house. The main bedroom will be taken over by the bride and groom, while the number one guest-room will be occupied by Rex and myself——'

Justin interrupted her. 'There'll be no need for any changes. Mary and I will not be living here.'

'*What*?' The room echoed with cries of dismay, and while the others looked at him wonderingly Rex demanded with impatience, 'Then tell us—where shall you be living? Don't tell me you'll be taking up residence in the city—driving back and forth each day.'

Justin laughed. 'Of course not. We'll be next door in the Grovers' house.'

There was another stunned silence, broken again by Rex, who turned to his wife. 'Laura, my dear—I'm afraid your nephew has gone slightly potty. His engagement to Mary is probably proving too much for him. Mind you, I don't blame him for going off his head a bit.'

Justin sent him an impish grin. 'Didn't I tell you I'd bought their place?' he queried nonchalantly.

'You know damned well that you didn't,' Rex exploded. 'When did this happen?'

'Today.' Justin's voice remained casual. 'I take over on the last day of next month. On that day, Rex, you may have the pleasure of removing the boundary fence.

It's what you've wanted to do for so long—despite thou shalt not covet thy neighbour's orchard.'

The old man's eyes gleamed. 'I'll see to it—personally.'

Laura turned to Elizabeth, her voice full of suppressed excitement. 'It's a lovely home. The kitchen's a dream, and from the upstairs windows there are views of the sea and the white cliffs of Young Nick's Head. Really—I feel so happy about it. Needless to say, I've been *hoping*, but nothing seemed to be *happening* between the pair of them.'

Justin said, 'I'll be taking Mary to see the house tomorrow—and to receive an apology from Rochelle. That much I insist upon.'

His words filled Mary with apprehension. She had no wish to see Rochelle again—ever. She couldn't care less about an apology from a person of her type—but she was longing to see the house where she would live with Justin.

It would be the house where they would rear their children, and as she visualised all that lay before her she was gripped by an eagerness that made her eyes shine. 'Yes—let's go tomorrow morning,' she said, her former apprehension switching to suppressed excitement.

'That's my girl,' Justin approved.

Next morning the sun was shining from a cloudless blue sky when Justin and Mary walked through the orchard towards the boundary fence. 'Welcome to our new world,' he said in a low voice as they climbed over the wires held by strainer-posts and battens.

The layout of the neighbouring property was similar to the Valencia, and while the recent wind had sent an equal amount of fruit to the ground there were still plenty of golden balls peeping from between the dark green leaves. They passed a tractor towing a grapefruit-laden trailer towards the packing shed, and they could hear the chatter of pickers who were up ladders.

'I presume you'll continue to employ them?' Mary whispered.

'Of course.'

'Their voices have a happy sound,' she commented.

However, the same could not be said of the voices issuing from within the house as they stood at the open front door. Nor did it take many moments to realise that Bob Grover was being berated by his wife and daughter.

'How *dare* you sell this property without consulting me?' Susan's voice raged at her husband.

'It happens to belong to me,' he shouted back at her. 'Have you forgotten we're going to the Gold Coast? I can't possibly run it from across the Tasman—or do you think I should try?' His voice had become scathing.

Rochelle shrieked above the arguments of her parents. 'Daddy, you *gave* the place to me. Mummy said so.'

'Damned rot—I did nothing of the sort,' he declared hotly. 'That was your mother's idea entirely—although it's easy to guess why she put such a rumour about the district, especially next door.'

'But I *want* to run the orchard,' Rochelle persisted in a loud and tearful voice. 'You and Mummy can go to the Gold Coast. I want to stay here. This is my home. I won't leave it.'

'Don't be stupid, Rochelle,' her father roared in exasperation. 'This asset is too valuable to leave in your hands. You've neither the ability nor the experience to run the place. You'd be down the drain in a very short time.'

At the front door Mary laid a hand on Justin's arm. 'We're eavesdropping,' she pointed out in a whisper.

'Yes. I'm finding it to be most interesting.' He raised his hand and pressed a button that sent musical chimes echoing through the house. They brought Rochelle to the door. She was followed by her mother, who in turn was followed by Bob Grover. The latter stood leaning against a door in the background, and Mary thought he looked thoroughly weary.

Rochelle's jaw sagged when she saw Justin and Mary. 'What do you want?' she demanded aggressively.

Justin gritted coldly, 'We'll begin with an apology from you to Mary—about you know what.'

'Go to hell.' Rochelle's voice was raised. She moved quickly, making an attempt to slam the door in their faces, but Justin's rapid action prevented her from doing so.

Susan stepped nearer. 'What is this about?' she demanded in a haughty tone. 'Why should my daughter apologise to—to *that girl*?'

Justin spoke icily. 'Because your daughter locked Mary in a shed and left her to be found whenever she was found. She could have suffered dire consequences.'

Rochelle paled visibly. 'That's a lie——' she began.

'I think not.' Justin's voice gritted with anger. 'The police were there when she was found. She has made a statement to them, and your fingerprints are likely to be on the door bar, as well as on my book of formulas. So—do you apologise or not?'

Rochelle took what she could see to be the wisest course. She apologised to Mary without sounding even remotely sincere about it.

Susan's voice shrilled. 'There now—I hope you're satisfied.'

Bob Grover came forward. 'He might be, but I'm not. I'd like to learn a few more details of Rochelle's activities.'

Justin said, 'I don't think you've met my fiancée.' He introduced him to Mary then added, 'If you'll walk home with us we'll show you the shed, and then you'll wonder why she doesn't press charges. But first she'd like to see through the house because this is where we'll live when we're married.'

His last words brought a shriek of rage from Rochelle. 'She will be living in our house? I can't bear it—I can't bear it——!' Sobbing loudly, she ran from the hall.

Susan Grover glared at Mary. 'If you think you can nose through this house you can think again,' she declared icily.

Mary spoke for the first time since Rochelle and her mother had entered the hall. Forcing a smile, she said sweetly, 'Very well, Mrs Grover—I quite understand your reluctance to allow me to see where Justin and I will live when we're married. I'm sure it's a lovely home, and I'm also sure we'll be very happy living in it.'

Bob turned upon Susan, his voice harsh. 'You're being completely brainless, my dear. I shall show Justin and Mary through the house whether you like it or not.'

He then took Mary's arm and led her into a spacious lounge that was joined to the dining-room by concertina doors that pushed back to the walls. As Laura had said, the kitchen was a dream, while the upstairs rooms looked upon pleasant views from every window. By the time they came downstairs Mary's sympathy was with Rochelle and her mother who would be leaving this lovely home.

After that Bob Grover walked with them to look at the shed. His careworn face was grave, and he was obviously shocked by the vicious action of his daughter. He could do little more than offer more apologies to Mary.

When he left them she said, 'I feel sorry for that man. I suspect he's downtrodden by his wife and daughter.'

'That's a fact,' Justin agreed. 'But now he has a weapon to use against them. In future, whenever war breaks out, he'll throw reminders of the shed at them.' He drew her into his arms then added, 'For the present you and I must forget about them, my darling. We still have a busy day ahead of us.'

'We have?' She looked at him expectantly. 'What have you in mind? Is it something exciting?'

'How would you rate driving to Gisborne to buy the best engagement ring we can find—followed by obtaining a marriage licence?'

'Oh, I can't think of anything more wonderful——'

'Can't you? I can,' he murmured, nuzzling her lips. 'That's only the beginning. I can't wait to make you my own darling wife.'

His words drew sighs of contentment from her as she returned his kisses. And as she clung to him she forgot the surroundings of the shed and its bags of fertiliser.

The horrors of her ordeal in it were swept from her mind while she recalled that this was the place where Justin had told her he loved her.

As the kiss ended he said, 'I'd like us to be married before your parents return to Sydney to attend to their affairs.'

She thought for a moment then began to giggle until her amusement changed to hearty laughter.

He shook her slightly. 'What's so funny? Don't you dare keep this joke from your future husband.'

She wiped tears of mirth from her eyes. 'Don't you see? My parents came to New Zealand to pack Gran's belongings and sell the house. Now they're returning to Sydney to pack their own belongings and sell the house.'

He chuckled. 'What makes you imagine I hadn't already seen that anomaly? It's one of the reasons I'd like us to be married as soon as possible. Our wedding is not to be delayed while your mother dithers over whether or not she'll keep items she hasn't used for years and years.'

Mary smiled. 'Believe me, Mother never dithers. Right now she's probably searching the shops for my wedding dress.'

'You mean a white gown and bridal veil with all the trimmings?'

She nodded. 'Everything she herself was unable to have, she'll want for me.'

'Like a wedding in the orchard? Have you noticed that our early oranges are blooming nicely? Give them a few more days and they'll be a mass of blossom.'

Mary looked at him with love shining from her eyes. 'Do you think it would be possible for us to be married there?'

Justin's arms tightened about her. 'For you, my dearest one, anything is possible.' He held her against him while kissing her long and deeply, then he put her from him with firm hands. 'Now we must move smartly because we have much to do in Gisborne. Nor must I neglect our travel arrangements.'

'Travel?' she queried in a daze, her heart thumping from the passion of his kiss and the knowledge that he wanted her.

'For our honeymoon. Would you prefer Fiji, Norfolk Island, or Hawaii? Yes—I think Hawaii will suit us nicely.'

Mary's mind was in a whirl as she thought of all that lay before her. Extreme excitement, mixed with an over-whelming happiness, made her unable to think clearly, and two hours later when Justin slipped a large solitaire on her finger she was almost speechless while dabbing at tears of joy.

When the day of their wedding dawned the sun shone warmly from the brilliant blue of a typical Gisborne dis-trict sky that was devoid of clouds. The pickers and packers from both orchards had combined in preparing a suitable area for the ceremony to take place, having chosen a stretch where the blossoms were most abundant and filled the air with perfume.

In fact they simply took over, organising where the trestle-tables were to be set, and where the drinks were to be served. They helped the caterers with food and champagne, and they conducted the parking of the many cars that arrived. Justin was delighted with their efforts and whispered to Mary that they would all get an extra bonus.

'They're not doing it for extra money,' Mary told him. 'They're doing it for *you*. It's a sign of their affection for you.'

She was delighted to see that Bob and Susan Grover were present, although there was no sign of Rochelle. But that mattered not one scrap because Rochelle had been eliminated from her mind. As far as Mary was con-cerned Rochelle no longer existed.

Eventually the time came for them to leave the party, and as they made their departure glasses were raised while voices shouted, 'To the orchard king—and his queen.'

Justin laughed as he swept Mary up into his arms and carried her towards the house.

Elizabeth made a move to follow them. 'I'll come and help Mary out of her dress,' she declared.

Justin swung round to face her. 'You'll remain at the party, I'll help Mary out of her dress.'

'But—I've acted as matron of honour,' Elizabeth argued.

'No matron of honour comes into the room while my wife and I are changing,' he informed her in a tone that was final.

From the shelter of Justin's arms Mary caught her father's eye. She giggled while he grinned and winked at her. They both knew that Elizabeth had met her match.

In the bedroom Justin crushed her against his heart. 'My darling bride—moon of my delight,' he said huskily. 'You're so beautiful—and I love you so very much.'

Mary looked at him shyly. 'Did I tell you I love you too? I can't count the exact number of ways.' She lifted the veil of filmy nylon from her head then released the sleeve fastenings at her wrists. 'Could you unzip me, please?' Then, as the dress fell about her feet in a mass of frothy white lace, Justin pushed aside straps to kiss her bare shoulders and breasts.

But suddenly he pulled himself together and, looking deeply into her eyes, he said, 'I shall love you forever, my orchard queen. Let's get started on our honeymoon...'

Where do you find hot Texas nights, smooth Texas charm and dangerously sexy cowboys?

COWBOYS AND CABERNET

Raise a glass—Texas style!

Tyler McKinney is out to prove a Texas ranch is the perfect place for a vineyard. Vintner Ruth Holden thinks Tyler is too stubborn, too impatient, too...Texas. And far too difficult to resist!

CRYSTAL CREEK reverberates with the exciting rhythm of Texas. Each story features the rugged individuals who live and love in the Lone Star State. And each one ends with the same invitation...

Y'ALL COME BACK...REAL SOON!

Don't miss *COWBOYS AND CABERNET* by Margot Dalton. Available in April wherever Harlequin books are sold.

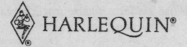

THE TAGGARTS OF TEXAS!

Harlequin's Ruth Jean Dale brings you
THE TAGGARTS OF TEXAS!

Those Taggart men—strong, sexy and hard to resist...

You've met Jesse James Taggart in FIREWORKS!
Harlequin Romance #3205 (July 1992)

And Trey Smith—he's THE RED-BLOODED YANKEE!
Harlequin Temptation #413 (October 1992)

And the unforgettable Daniel Boone Taggart in SHOWDOWN!
Harlequin Romance #3242 (January 1993)

Now meet Boone Smith and the Taggarts who started it all—
in LEGEND!
Harlequin Historical #168 (April 1993)

Read all the Taggart romances!
Meet all the Taggart men!

Available wherever Harlequin Books are sold.